AF231391

The Evelyn Thomas Chronicles
Book one of the Uriel's Army Saga
By R.M West

Text Copyright © 2017 R.M West
All Rights Reserved

*To my loving family for all your support and time.
This would never have happened without you all.*

Table of Contents

Chapter One

They're the deepest amber with a burst of fiery crimson in the centre, like the most beautiful gemstone I'd ever seen. Sometimes the crimson is so considerable it looks like the whole iris is consumed by it, and other times they're the smoothest of ambers that soothes me deep into my soul. They burn into me with so much power, they control me and I have no problems with obeying them. They feel like my life source, my destiny and I refuse to accept otherwise. They light fires deep inside me that no one else ever has, and I long for more. More than just eyes.

Well, that's while I'm asleep anyway. Once the cold light of day hits me it's a good hard slap from reality and I almost forget I've seen them, even though I've seen them every night since I was sixteen years old and that was some two hundred years ago now, two hundred and eighteen to be exact, but who's counting?

For 200 years I've been seeing those eyes and for well over a century I was obsessed, I refused to believe they weren't meant for me. But not once in all my years have I seen such eyes, not even close. So, I did what any self-respecting woman would do… I ignored it. I supressed my feelings and pretended it wasn't happening anymore, which I think my family greatly appreciated. I think they got pretty sick of me whining about my *"big amber eyes"* for over a century.

The elders of our community thought that I was observing my mate for a while, but they also got tired and after some time figured that I was just seeking attention.

So, I decided to keep quiet about it and now they just look at me like an old spinster. Two hundred and thirty-four years old and no mate, it's unheard of in my community: a woman of my age living at home with no family yet to speak of, or anytime soon by the looks of things, Maker forbid! But then I never was the same as everybody else here. I was sent down south as a baby when my family died, it was a terrible car accident and I managed to survive, nobody knew how, and I probably never would.

Here they all have similar powers and skills with some minor variations, where as I was totally different on that front. Although my powers are only mild as I won't fully bloom until I find my mate, I am noticeably stronger than most here, which I think makes them nervous, so I try to keep my full skillset under wraps as much as possible.

But, I haven't just spent the last two hundred years wallowing, I've built myself a remarkable business and I couldn't love it more. I own a very exclusive country club and resort about twenty miles from the settlement, and when I say exclusive, by that I mean it's exclusive to Mystics only, somewhere they can relax and be themselves and not worry about being seen by humans. It really is a magical place, literally, but also metaphorically. It absolutely hums with life and I adore it, I am so proud of what me and my team have accomplished there. It obviously comes with some minor dangers as some of our clientele are a little on the crazy mass murdering side, but hell, I'm not there to judge, just to keep the peace and the atmosphere serene. So far nothing other than a few brawls over some petty tennis games or a few bar fights over the succubae, has ever happened and we do our best to keep it that way. And for the most part we do a fantastic job. Mystics travel far and wide to come and stay with us and we make sure it's worth it. But, today is Sunday, and no matter what or who you are, in the south, you go to church on Sundays. In all fairness, ours is a slightly different kind of church. I mean the idea is the same, there's a "God" and we "pray" but just not how humans might imagine it to be. We celebrate instead. Our "God" we pray to is Mother Nature, also known as the Maker, and we worship nature because it's our life source, it's where our powers derive. So, we party, we drink, we dance, we make peace. It is a truly wonderful day for all of us and it's a day where it doesn't matter who you are or what you do because it's The Makers Day and all become unified in the eyes of The Maker.

Chapter Two

Luckily for me Makers Day doesn't mean Sunday best so I throw on some jeans and my favourite Tee and head downstairs. Halfway down I smell the sweet scent of momma's waffle iron and that means only one thing… Jimmy's home.

I fly down the stairs as fast I can, I can't wait to see him. It feels like it's been forever. I sail through the house and out onto to deck where I know he'll be lying on his hammock soaking up the southern sun.

Most of the year Jimmy works in Alaska as a tree surgeon so when he comes home it's all about the sunshine. Jimmy, for all intent and purposes is my big brother, except he isn't. Jimmy is a shapeshifter, a very common Mystic by today's standards and he was found as a baby by a clan up in Nebraska somewhere and sent here as they had trouble blending him in. You see Jimmy shifts into what you might perceive to be a black panther, he's a huge black cat type creature but closer to bear-size than panther-size and fluffier than your average panther, though I wouldn't recommend calling him fluffy.

His then surrogate family were beavers. Now as loving and friendly as beavers are, once Jimmy started to come into adulthood they couldn't blend him in anymore, he was just too big.

Shapeshifters tend to grow in human form to a similar-ish size as their Mystic form, with slight obvious differences. So, he was sent here, as there were already so many "lost young" here, as the elders like to call us, it made sense and he was also able to fit in a lot easier as an orphan. So, he is now and always will be my big brother and I loved him more than anyone or anything else in the world.

What a Sunday!

I practically leap across the garden and throw myself onto his hammock.

"'Bout time, Evie! I've been waitin' out here for hours," he roared as I send the hammock swinging, he had gotten even bigger than the last time he came home, the work must be building up some serious muscle because he was huge! He was scruffy as hell and looked like he needed a week of sleep, but he was home to me, and it was so good to see him.

We sat and chatted for a while, catching up on each other's lives etc., then after an hour or so Momma called from the kitchen and it was time for brunch, and a proper Makers Day brunch it was too; pancakes and waffles piled high, bacon, eggs, syrup, coffee, fresh juice, the smell of cookies and biscuits coming from the oven, I felt fifty years old again and I was in heaven.

We all sat down and ate together, all nine of us, just like the old days. There was Pops at the head of the table, he was a big Santa Clause looking fellow with a fluffy grey beard and still a full head of hair, which for his age was pretty impressive. He laughed his big old laugh and his happiness filled the whole house, it was such a wonderful thing to see. He loved nothing more than having us all home together. Momma was on his right, as always, and then the rest of us filled in around them, my big motely family of orphaned Mystics and their two adoring parents, what a wonderful sight!

After brunch, Anna-May and I washed the dishes while the others got ready for church, Anna-May was my youngest sister and our newest recruit. She was a shy girl with her head in the clouds, but she was a good egg. She loved nothing more than to sit outside under the sun, or moon, and daydream the day away. We talked and giggled about boys while we washed, I think she took to me more than the others because I didn't treat her like a child, even though she was nearly eighty and coming into adulthood I think everyone took her innocence as a sign of naivety, but I didn't see that. Anna-May was old beyond her years but in a very sweet and charming way, she was a hard one to describe I guess, but she's my baby sister and I love her nonetheless.

Just as we finished putting the dishes away Aimee, one of my other siblings and the only biological child of our parents, came rushing in to hand me my phone. "It's been buzzing like a cricket for ages", she said shoving it at me. "I thought one of the damned things had gotten in ma' room," she yelled as she run off to finish getting ready. When I looked down at my phone I saw I had 15 missed calls from Pierre. This couldn't be good; he would only call me on a Sunday if it was dyer.

Pierre was my second in command at The Lodge, he handles all the entertainment matters and was incredible at his job. He was a master conjurer in France and moved out here just to work with me at The Lodge. He puts on some of the most incredible shows you can imagine; it's helped along with a lot of magic, obviously, but that's not the point. The man is seriously talented and also one of my best friends. If he was phoning me on a Sunday it could only mean trouble. I snuck outside onto the deck for some privacy while I rung him back.

"Ah… I see you 'ave decided to grace me with a response to my endless frenzy of panicked messages, 'ow kind of you," he scoffed at me with his strong French accent dripping with nonchalant sarcasm.

"It's Sunday, Pierre, what's the problem?" I grumbled down the phone at him.

"Well, as you asked me so nicely, we're having a bit of a ta-do with the Alutiiq booking."

Crap! This was not good.

The Alutiiq booking could be an annual account for the rest of forever if we didn't mess it up. The Alutiiq's are the head family of the Ursidae Clans and every year they organise a gathering of the clans where every single member, and their friends, travel from all over the world to come together for one month to celebrate Samhain. You may know it as Halloween but to most of us, Samhain is the most significant night of the year. It's like Christmas, Birthdays, and all public holidays rolled into one. Apart from Sunday service, which is definitely not the same, it's the only time we actually celebrate together. Every year the different clans hold their own celebrations, but the Ursidae clans are the largest and by far the most powerful collective of clans around.

I suppose all being giant bear shifters has nothing to do with it.

Apart from the Council they were top of the food chain and if we got this right they would be flooding to us for a whole month every year for forever. We had to get this right.

"How can we be having a ta-do? Everything is set up to perfection for their arrival tomorrow. What possible trouble could we be having?" I stressed down the phone.

"Well now don't get your knickers in a twist wiz' me *Prinzess*! Ze problems we are 'aving is that they are 'ere, now. The First Lady and her kin arrived an hour ago and she has already slapped Sophia from reception, twice!"

No, no, no, no, no!

My heart stopped. How could this be? I took the booking myself they aren't due to arrive till nightfall tomorrow. Panic started to set in.

Okay think, Evelyn, think! How to fix this, how, how, how?

I stomped up and down the deck, my head swirling with possible ways to cater for them until tomorrow. We only have standard rooms left in the hotel for tonight and they would undoubtedly leave if I offered them those.

"THE HOUSE!" I squealed done the phone.

"The 'ouse?" he said and I could see the blank expression on his face through the phone.

"Yes the 'ouse," I mimicked, "my house. We can offer them their own private quarters until tomorrow when their rooms are ready." I was so satisfied with myself I was grinning from ear to ear.

My house was on the Lodge grounds and it was finished to the highest of standards. It was meant to be for me and my mate as a gift from the builders who built The

Lodge for me but I had never used it, it never felt right and if I ever needed to stay there I always used a room in the staff quarters.

"Give them everything they could possible need and I'll be there within the hour," I blurted out as I rushed indoors to change my clothes.

As I hung up the phone and rounded the bottom of the stairs, Jimmy was standing there a few steps up with his arms folded giving me that stupid big brother look he seemed to have perfected the moment we met all those years ago.

"Jimmy, no, don't do this. You know I wouldn't leave on a Sunday unless it was serious," I whined.

"Don't do what, Sis? I don't know what you mean," he said stamping his foot and giving me the 'butter wouldn't melt' face.

"I just have to go to work for a few hours to sort out a problem and then I'll be home, I promise," I put my hands together in a prayer like fashion to beg.

"I'm not stopping you from going, ya dumbass, I want you to take me with you," he whispered, "I am not sitting round here and churching it up without you."

"Oh, well then what are we standing here for?" I demanded. "Get upstairs and make yourself look pretty coz I'm gonna need you to turn the charm up to eleven today." I winked at him and flew past him up the stairs.

Once upstairs I throw on my best business attire. It was a black form-fitting dress with small vertical pinstripes and a built-in belt. It wasn't overly flashy but it looked expensive and it definitely hugged all the right things in all the right places. I slipped on my cost-me-a-pay-check stilettos, whipped my long auburn hair up in a quick French bun, threw on some makeup and flew downstairs.

When I reached the front porch, Jimmy was already explaining to everyone that I had a major emergency at work and needed his help with some tough clients. He had a way of making people really buy into whatever he was pedalling them at the time, one of his gifts I guess. They all looked up at me with such pitying looks on their faces, this would have gone very differently if it had been me who told them we were leaving. Mar and Pops gave us both a hug and told us to be careful, and we left.

Chapter Three

Jimmy made me put the top down on the way to The Lodge, he loved the sun so much he couldn't bear to miss a second of it. He laid his head back on the seat and sang aloud to the radio. Seeing him like this made my heart swell. He was so happy and looked like he needed the down time.

After a while we turned down the driveway to The Lodge, I say driveway it was more like a long private road that was enchanted to the max, as was the rest of the perimeter. We'd needed to make sure that no human or uninvited guests could find the resort or its location. I pulled round to the back service entrance and parked in my usual spot.

As soon as we stepped out of the car Pierre appeared ready to start his onslaught of moaning, but I pulled my secret weapon on him, Jimmy. As soon as he saw him his face lit up with the happiest of smiles and immediately raised his arms to welcome Jimmy home. No matter what mood someone was in, as soon as they saw Jimmy all was right with the world. Another one of his gifts. I eyed to Jimmy to keep Pierre busy while I sorted things out, he gave me a wink and brought Pierre in for a hug and I slinked off.

Once inside I headed straight for my office to grab all the info I needed on the Alutiiq's booking and then made a beeline for the hospitality offices. I wanted them to make sure the house was spotless and to make certain that the Alutiiq's would have everything they needed and more. They assured me it would be done and I trusted them as if I were doing it myself. Pixies had a knack for doing everything perfectly.

Once everything was underway I headed to the front desk to find Sophia and check the details of what happened, and where they were waiting. Sophia informed me that they had been given free reign of the resort to try and appease their troubles and that Lady Alanjula was last seen in the tennis bar with some of her "Gorillas", as Sophia described them. I checked myself in the full length mirrors on the walls behind reception, just to make sure I was presentable and headed for the tennis courts.

Once I entered the bar area it wasn't difficult to spot them. A group of extremely large men dressed in the finest attire sat and stood around. A blonde woman of incredible beauty and authority sat at one of the tables at the far end of the bar overlooking the tennis courts. She was talking in a dialect I didn't recognise but she sounded rather annoyed to say the least. I took in a deep breath and readied myself to transform into business mode. As I approached the table two large men stood in front of me and stopped me from passing. I had to tilt my head back to look them in the eye. I'm 5', 6" and even in my stilettoes they towered over me. This however was nothing new in my line of work or my life, I was always coming up pretty short when it came to Mystics, as a human woman no one wouldn't assume me anything other than average but compared to most Mystics I was petite and compared to these guys I might as well be an ant.

I think they could probably squish me just as easy as one as well.

But I was used to giant "Gorillas" trying to intimidate me with their size, it barely fazed me anymore. I looked at them both softly in the eyes and smiled my sweetest smile.

"Good afternoon, Gentlemen, it's a pleasure to meet you both." I stuck out my hand to shake theirs but they just stared blankly at me so I carried on. "I am Evelyn Thomas the manager here at The Lodge and I've come to see if we can't get this mess sorted for you all as soon and as smoothly as possible." As I finished my introduction I squeezed between the two men I felt one of them go to grab me but with a wave of my hand I froze him where he stood, he tried to groan slightly in protest. I twirled on my heels to face them. "Let's get this straight from the get go shall we, Gentlemen? You play nice or ya'll have to leave, is that clear?" I gave another sweet smile, winked at the one that wasn't frozen and sauntered off to meet Lady Alanjula as the free one burst out laughing and mocking his frozen friend.

As I reached the table a tall blonde man who sat opposite the first lady rose to address me.

"Ah, you must be, Miss Thomas?" he held out his hand to greet me. I extended my hand out to meet his but instead of shaking it he took it gently in his hand, raised it to his mouth and pressed a delicate kiss just above my knuckles.

Well that's new…

I quickly composed myself and smiled sweetly.

"I am indeed and it's a pleasure to meet you, Mr Alutiiq I presume?"

"Oh please, Ma'am, call me Charlton," he said offering me a seat as he sat back down opposite Lady Alanjula at which point she let out an exasperated huff.

"For Maker's sake, Charlton, this woman is not your friend. Have her address you properly, Boy."

I looked between the two of them, my first thought was that it must have been his mother but even though she looked young and beautiful she was definitely much older than him and me, possibly the both of us put together. My best guess would be grandmother.

Maker, she's going to be hard work.

I turned back to Charlton, "It would be an honour, Charlton, thank you," I said grinning as he stifled a laugh.

"And you must be the, Honourable First Lady Alanjula? It's an honour and a pleasure to finally meet you and I do hope we can put this terrible misunderstanding behind us?" She doesn't respond so I just carry on. "I am Evelyn Thomas, the manager here at The Lodge and I will be doing everything I can to make sure your stay here is as good as it can be from this moment on." I looked at her smiling waiting for a response. She eventually let out a small sigh and looked up at me.

"Well I don't know if I must be but yes, I am Lady Alanjula, and that is how you shall address me," she said giving Charlton a sniping side look. "I should like you to know that I have been less than impressed with the treatment we have had so far and at this point I am considering cancelling the entire event. Our welcoming here has been far less than satisfactory and I don't see how you will rectify it adequately." She now sat facing me and looked up at me with a particularly smug look on her face.

"My deepest and sincerest apologies to you all, Lady Alanjula. I do sincerely hope that you can see fit to forgive me for not having your accommodation ready a day earlier than you booked. I promise to do everything in my power to make the rest of the day as easy as possible and have arranged some luxury accommodation for you until your rooms are ready tomorrow at nightfall, when you originally planned to arrive." My digs and blatant finger pointing didn't go unnoticed but before she could respond I continued in my sweet and silky-smooth work voice. "I also feel I should add… I have been informed that at some point today one of your party assaulted my receptionist, Sophia. If this were to happen again I'm afraid your entire party would be asked to leave and the events would be cancelled immediately. We, here at The Lodge, have a no tolerance policy to violence, towards anyone, but especially the members of staff and that does not exclude anyone regardless of who they are." She looked as though she may either die of embarrassment or kill me for the insult, but I didn't want to sit around to find out which it would be, so before she could react I smiled the biggest smile I could and then clapped my hands together as my pager had gone off in my pocket letting me know that the house was ready. "But…" I say holding my hands up, "leaving that sour note behind us, your accommodation is ready for you all, so if you'd like to follow me?" I got up and started for the exit. I felt a lot of hustle and bustle start behind me so I assumed they were following.

As I got to "Mr Grabby", the man I had frozen earlier, I touched his arm so he could move again and leaned in to whisper "I trust there will be no more concerns between us?" He just nodded in response so I gave him a fabulously big grin and went on my way.

As I got to the door I turned to wait for them to catch up with me and I saw Charlton approaching.

"Well played, Miss Thomas, you must tell me how you have a pair big enough to talk to her like that, and let me know where you got them," he said laughing as he reached me, "I must say that's not something I have ever seen in all my 400 years and I don't think she has either." He was now grinning at me from ear to ear.

He really was a beautiful man. Thick blonde hair that swept silkily across his forehead and he had the brightest brown eyes I had ever seen, they almost glowed. He was well built and by the way his suit fit him he was also incredibly muscular under there as well.

Now, now, Evelyn. Keep it professional.

"Oh my apologies, I never intended to offend anyone but we have very strict rules here that I can't allow to be broken," I said as nicely as I could.

"No, no! No offense taken at all. I think you did amazingly, Miss Thomas," he stroked my arm, "keep up the good work." He winked at me before leaving my side to assist his group with all the luggage.

He's definitely going to be trouble.

I march as quickly as I can across the resort taking the long way round so they didn't have to walk past the service entrances, I didn't think that would go down to well. There were a few remarks from her Ladyship about the distance it was from the rest of the resort but I assured her it was worth the distance and we would arrange for transport for them was it required.

As we turned the corner at the edge of the woodlands a large plot opened out and there she was. Every time I saw this house it made my heart swell with such an overwhelming sense of joy, it was hard to describe. I felt like it was a joy I hadn't experienced yet but couldn't wait to either. I let them all catch up to me so they could take in the beauty of her. As they arrived I feel them all take her in and they were not disappointed. I got a few impressed grunts and groans and even her ladyship didn't have any complaints.

"Well here we are," I said gesturing up to the house. "If you would like to follow me I'll give you the grand tour."

I lead everyone into the reception hall and showed them a large closet in case they wanted to store any luggage or such like, before carrying on. We went first to the kitchen which was finished with magnificently glossy cream cabinets that lined the back wall of the room in a U-shape, with top and bottom cabinets running most of the way and full length floor to ceiling cabinets at the far end. The countertop was a dark polished marble that glistened with newness.

I don't think this kitchen has ever been used. Such a shame.

On the other side of the vast room, in front of a wall that consisted mainly of giant windows that looked out over the woodlands, sat a large ten seater dining table that had been set up beautifully with crystal cut glasses and the finest of china.

I knew I could count on my team to go the extra mile.

Everything was seamless and finished to the highest of standards. It looked like it belonged in a celebrity home you might see on T.V. and the rest of the house didn't disappoint either. There was a large sitting room that could easily cater for the 14 of them here and possibly a few more if they arrived, there was a games room and cinema room on the basement level and another dinning and sitting room here on the first floor. At the end of the hallway it opened out into a large garden room full of beautiful furniture, that you wouldn't be surprised to find in a boutique lounge. The back wall of the room was made completely of bi-folding glass that opened fully onto the porch decking and down to the back yard. Which was of course perfectly landscaped.

Up on the second floor there were four master bedrooms all with en-suites and walk in closets and we had also added extra beds and partitions to most of the rooms, to cater for its current occupants. On the third floor there were three further rooms that were supposed to be used as offices and day nurseries but we had turned them into extra rooms for our unexpected guests.

Once I had given them the grand tour I made sure they had a list of contacts, including myself, and told them if they needed anything at all they just needed to contact the appropriate numbers and they would be taken care of.

I said my final apologies and goodbyes and made my way out.

As I got to the end of the path Charlton called to me from the front door. He was jogging up behind me putting on his jacket. "If you don't mind, Miss Thomas, I'd like to escort you back to the main building?" he said as he came up beside me.

"Please call me, Evelyn, and you may of course but there is honestly no need." I smiled at him as he looked at me with a look I couldn't quite figure out but as soon as it had come it had gone and he started to move us forward.

"Well if I must be honest, Evelyn, I need to head back anyway. I have to find my brother, we left him wondering around the resort, so he might be wondering where we've got to." He offered me his arm and we strolled back to the resort chatting and laughing along the way. He was an incredibly charismatic man and was, to be honest, a complete joy to be around. I rarely found someone I liked as quickly as I did him and it was a pleasure.

The dreamy, suave rich prince type thing he had going for him didn't hurt either.

Chapter Four

When we finally reached the main building I found Sophia outside waiting for her ride home. I said my goodbyes to Charlton and went to wait with her.

"So I get slapped in the face, twice! And you get sunset walks with, Mr Salty-Goodness over there? Fricking typical," she moaned. I giggled, I couldn't help myself, Sophia had a way about her that just made me laugh. She was so sweet and seemingly innocent but was most definitely not!

She checked her watch and was getting fidgety. Nightfall was coming and Sophia was our only human employee. It wasn't something we did regularly but Sophia grew up in our world so none of this was a shock or new information to her, but we made sure that she never worked past sunset. She could take care of herself and this place was mainly as safe as it got, but for a human it got pretty scary here after dark, and I didn't blame her for wanting to get away especially after the day she'd had.

I grabbed my phone and called Jimmy asking him to meet me out the front with the car.

After a few minutes later he pulled round and I told him to take Sophia home and then head back himself. I'd need to be here tonight anyway, in case her Ladyship or one of her kin needed something or wanted to complain some more. Sophia and Jimmy tried to protest to my staying there alone but I put my foot down and they eventually gave in.

Once back in the main building I checked around a bit to make sure none of today's dramas had upset any other guest but all seemed to be fine. I finally headed to my office to find Pierre and tell him he could finish up early. He needed the rest as tomorrow didn't look like it would be any easier than today and he certainly didn't put up a fight when I sent him home. We said our goodbyes and off he went to his quarters.

Once he was gone I plonked in the chair behind my desk, slid my shoes off and got stuck into some paperwork and pre-party checks for the weeks ahead. The last thing we needed was more hiccups so we really had to make sure all ran smoothly over the next few weeks.

A few hours must have past and I had been starring at the same piece of paper for a good twenty minutes now so decided a break would be a good idea. It was already nearly midnight and no one had rung or kicked up a fuss so far, so I was hopeful we might get through the night with some peace. I grabbed myself a bottled water from my stash and laid back on the couch I had in my office. It was a home away from home for me this thing, it had seen me through many an evening of stressful times and sleepless nights here at The Lodge, especially in the early days. I thought if I could get a few minutes of down time I would be as good as new to power through in an hour or so and before I knew it I was asleep.

They were brighter and stronger than ever. My beautiful amber eyes burning into me like beacons calling to me. But this time something was different, there was more, but I couldn't quite figure out what.

I tried to reach out to him, to touch him as I did every night and never could, but this time it was different. He still had no body to speak of but I could feel him more than ever and I could see a bit more than just eyes. Not a full face, just more.

I was also sure I could see hair, thick black hair. I felt myself being pulled in closer and closer to him. Again, being commanded to obey. As I got close enough I tried to really study him. Suddenly his face starts to reveal itself, bit by bit he was showing himself to me.

"WHAT THE FUCK IS YOUR PROBLEM, C? HUH? WHY DO YOU FUCKING CARE SO MUCH ABOUT WHO SHE IS?"

I awoke with a start, jumped up and ran to my office door. The commotion in the lobby was so loud I had to stop it immediately. I even forgot to put my shoes on in the panic.

I ran out to find Charlton and another man I hadn't yet met, shouting at each other in the middle of the main lobby. Well, more like growling at each other in the middle of the lobby. It must have been the early hours as the hotel was silent apart from them and I knew people would start showing up soon and that wasn't acceptable.

"Gentlemen please," I called as I marched towards them. "It is too late and you are too loud! This cannot go on in here!" I demanded but as I got a bit closer to them Charlton turned to look at me with a mix of surprise and horror. I assumed he may not have expected me to still be here but I was still taken aback by his look and it stopped me in my tracks. The other man closed his eyes and took a breath.

"Is that it?" he said as he started to laugh still staring at Charlton, a laugh that sounded cruel and somehow I was offended but I didn't know why.

"For fuck sake, Charlton. Is that what all this is about?" he bellowed. "Are you fucking kidding me? You think that some half-pint whore is the answer? You are in so much deeper than I thought, man… get your head out of your fucking ass. There is no way some little-"

"ENOUGH!" I yelled across the lobby.

Charlton spun to look at me in shock and what I assumed must have been his brother, just stopped. His chest heaving with rage.

"You will continue this somewhere else, Gentlemen. You are not the only guest in my hotel and I will not have you disrupting them anymore!" I said as calmly as I could manage but I pretty much spat it at them.

Charlton started to walk towards me with an apology spreading across his face but I just raised my hands and stopped him where he stood. For some reason I felt personally hurt and offended by their argument and I wanted to cry, I obviously didn't but if he started apologising I wasn't sure I could hold it back. I composed myself before I spoke. "If you would both kindly return to your quarters, Gentlemen, we can discuss this tomorrow when everyone has calmed down. I understand that this time of year can be stressful to all of us but that does not excuse this kind of behaviour. Your party has been warned once about your conduct in this hotel, I do not expect to have to mention it again."

Charlton gave me a stiff nod and turned to his brother, I could feel he was about to start up again so with a click of my fingers I magically sent him back to his quarters. Charlton looked around in shock.

"I am truly sorry for that, Mr Alutiiq, but I cannot allow him to disrupt my guests any more than he already has."

"What did you do with him?" he looked at me completely stunned.

"He is back at your quarters and if you would be so kind as to pass on my apologies for this evening I will formally apologise to him myself tomorrow," I said as nicely as I could and added a tight smile to finish it off. He just nodded, still stunned I think, but I didn't have it in me to wait around for a reply. I said goodnight and headed for the staff quarters.

Chapter Five

The next morning came all too quickly. As soon as the sun was up, so was I. I made myself a large strong coffee and headed for my office.

I had to use my emergency clothes I kept at the hotel for the time being as I hadn't planned to stay the night. I was wearing an old black dress of mine, it still looked expensive and I still looked good in it, but today I felt like I needed something a little extra to get me through it. I'd arranged for Jimmy to bring some clothes down later so I would have to wait 'till then and make do in the meantime.

When I got to my office Pierre was already working and had conjured up breakfast as well, "'Elp yourself, Princess," he smiled at me as I hovered over the beautiful French pastries that smelt like hot butter and freshly baked bread. I didn't need to be told twice, I stuffed a mouthful of a hot, chocolate filled pastry into my mouth and it was heaven. I'd forgotten how long it had been since I'd last eaten, I was starving, and Pierre's pastries were even better than his entertainment. I savoured the flavour of my oversized mouthful and flopped on the couch next to the desk.

"So I assume you 'ad a good night then?" Pierre said as I stuffed another bite of pastry into my mouth. I smiled at him as best as I could with a mouthful, "you could say that," I squeezed out between the food. I spent the next few minutes explaining what had happened the previous night and some bits from the day portion that he missed as well. Just as I finished and stuffed the last piece of pastry into my mouth there was a knock at the door. My eyes bulged out of my head, my mouth was so full I couldn't even speak. I ran into the bathroom just in time to hear Pierre to say "Entrez". The door opened and I heard someone come and start speaking in French.

This was new.

After I finished my mouthful I composed myself and went back to the office, to my surprise Charlton was stood in the doorway chatting away to Pierre in perfect French. "Ah, just the lady I was looking for," he beamed at me.

"Good morning, Mr Alutiiq, what can we do for you?" I said in my perfect business voice.

"Charlton, please," he pleaded. I just smiled at him. "I have come to express my apologies for last night and our behaviour in your home. I do not wish to dwell on the matter but if there is anything I can do to make it up to you I sincerely hope you'll let me?" he said with the sincerest look on his face.

"Thank you very much for your apology, Charlton, but there's no need. But I do trust it will not happen again?" I gave him the best stern mother look I could muster and even looked over my glasses at him. He beamed an incredible smile at me and came over and swept me up in a big hug.

This was also new.

He let me go and turned to say something in French to Pierre, to which he chuckled at more than politely, and then he turned to leave.

"Oh before I go," he said as he reached the door and turned to smile at me, "the family and I are having a small gathering tonight on the roof terrace to kick off the Samhain celebrations, just us, before everybody else gets here. It would be an honour if you could join us."

Well that threw me.

I looked at him open mouthed for a moment before correcting myself with a smile. "That is a very generous offer, Charlton, but I feel it would be inappropriate for me to join you as a guest, but if I haven't had a chance beforehand then I will be sure to stop by and apologise to your brother for my actions last night." I smiled and turned back to the desk to busy myself expecting that to be the end of conversation but he continued to stare at me. When I looked up he had the saddest look on his face. "I'm sorry, I didn't mean any offense by not accepting your offer I just-"

He cut me off raising his hand and shaking his head. "Miss Thomas, please, after our performance last night why on earth would you need to apologise to us? Especially my brother? He was out of line last night and you did what was required of you and no more. You acted very professionally and had everyone's best interests at heart. If anything he owes you an apology." He let out a heavy sigh and hung his head. "Please, Miss Thomas, try not to judge my brother too harshly." He raised his eyes to meet mine. They were full of sorrow and something I couldn't quite read. "He is not himself lately and this time of year is particularly hard on him. If you can find it in your heart to forgive him for last night I am sure he will make it up to you one day."

I took a moment to absorb what he said. "Of course I can." I forced the sweetest smile I could, "and if I get the time I will see you tonight," I said trying to hurry the end of the conversation that had suddenly made me feel very uncomfortable. He smiled broadly at me and left closing the door behind him.

"Well…. Zat was *very* interesting," Pierre smirked whilst staring at me over the top of his glasses.

I flushed a deep shade of crimson, "what do you mean?" I tried to keep my embarrassment out of my voice but who was I kidding.

Pierre stared at me for a while letting me squirm under his scrutiny, "well, well, well, Princess, I don't 'sink I've ever seen you get flustered like that by anyone before. Not even the succubae have that effect on you."

"That was really strange though, wasn't it?" Pierre just raised his eyebrows at me and went back to his paperwork, but there was definitely something odd about our conversation. I couldn't put my finger on what it was, but I felt there was more to it than what was being said.

Chapter Six

Our little meeting this morning stuck with me all day. I tried to busy myself so I didn't have time to dwell on it, but it didn't really help. I couldn't shake the odd feelings I'd got during it, it was almost like they weren't my own. I'd gone backwards and forwards with the idea of going to their party tonight and I'd finally landed on the idea of going. I figured it would show willing and that there was no hard feeling about the last twenty-four hours. However, if I was going I'd need to be dressed a lot better than this, and I'd need to get a handle on my emotions before I got there. I couldn't spend the entire evening inside my own head. I agreed with Pierre to let him dress me for tonight and asked Jimmy to accompany me, just for the support more than anything and so I could spend some time with him.

But first, I needed to calm myself down and ready my mind for whatever may happen tonight, after all, I'm not exactly in most of their good books currently, so best to be prepared, and there was only one way I did that.

Nearly two hundred years ago I took up the art of tai-chi, it sounds somewhat outlandish, but it really helps me control my energies, and has really helped me bond with my power. When I was much younger I had a lot of trouble controlling them and had a lot of accidents, even some where people got hurt, so I had to learn how to centre myself and tai-chi was what worked for me. I used my methods regularly so had a little place set up for myself in the woodlands we had on site. No one understood why I didn't just have a room set up somewhere in the hotel, but I craved the contact with the earth and nature. She was my source, my power, and being submerged in here beauty in the woods by a small stream was all I needed to calm and recharge. So when tai-chi was added to the equation, I was in paradise.

I changed into my exercise kit, which only consisted of a pair of very short cycling shorts and a cropped sports top. The more exposed I was the more I could channel my power. If I thought no one would ever see me I'd do it naked. So I grabbed my stuff and told Pierre where I'd be and headed out to what everyone else called the Thomas Spot, very original I know.

Walking across the resort everything looked beautiful, the sun was about an hour away from setting and was lighting up the sky with its bright and golden fall glow. The woodlands were starting to get a little dark so torches were lighting the way as I walked. We had them enchanted to come on for people as they passed so they didn't burn all the time. I could hear my spot before I reached it, I felt like it was calling to me. The sound of the running stream with its mini waterfall was music to my ears, I could feel myself recharging and feeling better already. When I reached it my usual picnic blanket and set of torches were out and lit waiting for me. I set my things down and slipped my trainers off so I could feel the grass under my feet and headed for the stream. I couldn't help it, I had to really centre myself and that meant water. It was calming to feel the stream rushing past my ankles and feet, it wasn't deep at all but deep enough to calm me and sooth my soul. I closed my eyes and let my head tilt back and absorb the last few rays of the day's sun and when I felt my power spring to life I knew it was time.

I needed a power surge today, to really make sure my energies were on a full charge, and today I felt like fire would give me the boost I needed. I could take energies from all the elements but today I felt the flames of the torches calling to me. I went over to the one with the biggest flame and held my hand above it, its heat was so inviting and peaceful and it never burns me. I asked the flame to join me and it reached up and formed a perfect glowing ball in my hand. I let it get used to me for a moment, staying very still I felt its force explore my body and once it was settled I headed for my blanket.

Tai-chi was a form of martial arts but it was slow and steady and wasn't about fighting or defence it was about energies and inner calm. I moved slow and steady through my movements allowing the fire to move within me wherever it wanted to go. I used the natural course of the flames to control my actions and let them restore me. I was lost in the exercise for some time when the flames started to react strangely. Something wasn't right, like a predator was approaching or something. I tried to reassure them but they were on the defensive. My whole body burst into bright blue flames and turned towards the threat. My eyes scanned every inch of the surrounding woodlands but there was nothing, no one, not even an animal and the breeze was still. It was completely calm, too calm. My eyes closed and my body stilled, I focused in on what was around me, I sent my energies out to explore the area and suddenly a small spark ignited deep in the vegetation ahead of me. There they were. Two bright glowing eyes staring back at me. My body froze, was I awake? Was I imagining them? I tried to concentrate but all I could feel was these eyes burning into me. They were the deepest amber, with a burst of crimson in the centre, like the most beautiful gemstone I'd ever seen. I could not believe what I was seeing. My heart pounded and my breath hitched in my throat. My flames turned to a gentle simmer and a calming orange colour and eventually went back to the palms of my hands. I stood unable to move staring at my big amber eyes. Suddenly my phone started ringing from my bag, the break in the eerie silence startled me and my head darted in the direction of it. Once I realised it was just my phone I turned back to find my eyes but they were gone. I wanted to run into the trees to find them but something stopped me, I couldn't feel them anymore, they were long gone. I stood for some time starring at the trees where they had been trying to decide if I was finally losing my mind or if I actually saw them. My phone eventually rang again and I knew it would be Pierre ringing to tell me off as it was getting late. I took one last paddle in the stream to try and loose the tension I had now gained from the experience and it helped but not enough. I let my flame go back to its torch and I left to find Pierre.

Once I had hunted down Pierre he had already got hold of Jimmy and dressed him in the finest casual suit I had ever seen and sorted his hair and shoes, he looked incredible. And with him in full charm mode I felt like I might actually get through the evening in one piece.

"Wow! You don't look like an under-payed lumberjack. What happened?" I teased him.

"Aw, thanks, Sis. Wish I could say the same!" he smirked.

Pierre gave a look of utter disgust and closed his eyes. I could only imagine what I looked like after my little incident down at the stream.

"Woman, please. At least try and give me *something* to work with." He let a dramatic sigh and waved his hands over me as if he were conducting music and then stood back with the biggest smile I'd seen on his face in weeks. "See…. She should let me dress her all the time, no?" he said to Jimmy.

"Well, Sis, he's not wrong. You look smoking," he said and let out a small whistle.

I blushed but smiled, this was exactly how I need to feel tonight. I bit my bottom lip out of habit and went over the mirror, I was in shock. With nothing more than a wave of his hands Pierre had transformed me from: I've been jogging in a fire pit, to: I am Cinder-fricking-rella and I shall go to the ball.

I had on a black full length cocktail dress that shimmered like it was covered in black diamonds. It had a crawl V-neck that showed off just the beginning of my cleavage and thin black straps so I was pretty bare up top. It had a long slit in the side that went up to my mid-thigh and exposed my leg and shoes. They matched the dress flawlessly. They were long healed, shimmering black stilettoes that looked like they cost more than my house and they fit me perfectly. They also made my now tanned legs look incredible. He'd fixed my hair into a beautiful up do and I'm pretty sure not all of it was mine, but it looked fabulous so who cares. My make-up was done to perfection but very subtle and classy. It was all finished off with a dazzling diamond necklace and a small clutch bag that matched the dress also. I was a tiny bit overwhelmed but I loved it nonetheless.

"Do we think this might be a little bit over the top for a roof terrace party?" I said still starring at myself in the mirror. "It is only the pool bar after all."

"No, darling, I made sure I knew what everyone was wearing before I dressed the two of you. They're all in their Sunday best, your best is just better." He winked at me and held his hand to me waiting for something. I looked at him confused.

"Your pager, Princess. Now!" he demanded.

"Oh no, really, Pierre, that won't be necessary, really."

He stamped his foot and shoved his hand at me, I gave in. There was no way I was winning this one.

Pick your battles, Evie.

So we were now all dressed and ready go, not to mention a bit more than fashionably late we headed for the terrace.

Chapter Seven

I was bit nervous to say the least, but I didn't really know why. The whole way there Jimmy kept asking if I was alright and what was wrong with me. I assumed he could feel me putting off some strange energies but I didn't know how to begin to explain what I felt so I just insisted I was fine.

Once we were outside ready to go up, he grabbed me and pulled me in for a big hug and pushed all of his good energy into me.

"No, Jimmy, you really don't need to do this, I'm okay, really." I tried to convince him I was fine and mainly get him to stop as I could feel eyes watching me and wasn't sure who they belonged to. But he knew me too well.

"Don't be a wiener, Evie, just take it and let it help get you through the night, it's not like I need it… I'm already fabulous," he joked as he stepped away and held me at arm's length to check how I looked. "You're pretty fabulous yourself, baby girl." He gave me wink, took my arm and turned to climb the stairs.

I could still feel eyes watching my every move but I couldn't pinpoint where they came from. As we reached the top of the stairs a few of the other hotel guests were at the bar area and greeted me with big smiles and fond "hellos" and mostly all of them were checking out the eye candy on my arm. I know he's my brother but you couldn't deny the effect he had on people, they were drawn to him… all of them.

As we approached the bar Jimmy moved forward to order us drinks and I gave myself a mental check over and tried to convince myself that we could have a good evening and just enjoy ourselves when I felt someone behind me.

"Well, Miss Thomas, you're positively glowing. You look radiant, my Darling, you really do. Ah and you brought a date." He looked slightly shocked and a little peeved if I wasn't mistaken, but he still had the same reaction as most people did to Jimmy. Especially when Jimmy turned and flashed him a dazzling smile.

"Oh, my apologies, Mr Alutiiq, this is my brother, Jimmy Thomas. He's home for Samhain so I thought I would bring him along. I hope that's okay?" I moved on not waiting for the reply. "Jimmy this is, Charlton Alutiiq. One the most refined guests we have had the pleasure of staying at The Lodge."

"Ah, your brother," Charlton said whilst he shook Jimmy's had with the biggest smile on his face.

I wasn't sure if Jimmy had made an impression or if he was relieved that he wasn't my date. We stood and spoke with Charlton for a while and he introduced us to a few people that came over to greet him. I finally started to relax. Charlton and Jimmy were both so comfortable and charming it was too difficult to resist them, even though I could still feel eyes watching me the entire time and the only eyes I could imagine were bright amber and glowing.

After a time and a few drinks Charlton clapped his hands together and gestured for my arm. "Would you care to dance, Miss Thomas? I adore this song."

I checked with Jimmy who gave me the, if you don't I will nod and off I went.

Charlton moved me around the floor like a professional. He was so fluid and smooth with his movements and managed to help me keep up with him as well. Although I'm not really sure how. I was generally a very average dancer but he made me look wonderful. Once his song finished it was followed by a much slower calming piece of music. He pulled me into him and slowly whirled us around the dancefloor in a delicate pattern.

"So how have you been today, Miss Thomas? I trust today was somewhat easier than yesterday?" He smirked down at me as I looked up to meet his gaze. He was honestly quite breath-taking. I searched his eyes for a moment, I couldn't help myself, I wanted to see if they were the eyes from earlier, my eyes. But alas they were not; beautiful, but they were not the eyes from earlier, or my dreams. They did, however, seem very familiar to me.

Odd.

"Looking for something?" he said with an odd expression on his face.

"Sorry, I didn't mean to stare at you, but your eyes are oddly familiar to me. I was trying to figure out why." I couldn't seem to stop staring at them like they might tell me what I need to know.

Suddenly my body felt an explosion of anger. It startled me and Charlton froze us both on the dancefloor. In the same second a deafening roar erupted from over by the bar followed by the attack cry of a panther.

Jimmy!

I darted across to where the roars had come from and Jimmy was hunched over in a defensive stance and another man was practically on all fours looking ready to pounce on Jimmy. Jimmy readied himself for impact as the other man transformed into a giant black bear and lunged for Jimmy. He quickly threw himself out of the way. The bear was enormous but luckily Jimmy was quicker. The bear continued to lunge for him but he refused to shift. He was trying to talk him round. "Come on, man. I don't understand what the problem is?" he was shouting as he tried to duck out of the way of the bears advances. I was starting to panic now, one false move and that bear would kill Jimmy. I was about to intervene when suddenly the bear jumped at Jimmy and they both went over the edge of the terrace. As soon as there was impact I heard a feral roar come from Jimmy and I knew he had shifted.

This is bad.

Two full grown shifters trying to knock ten shades of shit out of each other for no reason was a definite no-no.

And one of the idiots had to be my brother.

I saw Charlton start to remove his tie with intention of shifting as well.

"Don't you dare!" I screamed at him.

"He'll kill him!" he shouted at me with such dread in his eyes.

I ran for the stairs and flew down them as fast as I could. As I turned the corner of the building to where they had been fighting I was met dead in the face with bright glowing red eyes, and they were pissed. The energy coming off of this bear was unreal, but it just stared into me. I tucked the corner of my bottom lip between my teeth, I wasn't sure how to respond. It was almost amusing to see a giant bear with a look of surprise on its face. He was covered in cuts and blood. Jimmy, now in full panther form, landed on the floor next to me to try and get between me and the bear. This seemed to set the bear of again. I panicked and before either of them could do any actual damage I knocked them both unconscious with a wave of my hand. I'd managed to perfect the move over the years. It usually came in handy, running a place like this.

They fell to the floor with ground shaking thuds and transformed back into their human forms. As soon as the fight was over an eruption of loud howls, roars, cheers, and laughter broke out from the audience back up on the roof terrace behind us. With a few comments about how Samhain had really started, thrown in. I was of course mortified about their perverse enjoyment of the brawl but at least no one was offended by it. I quickly ran over to Jimmy to check his wounds but he was already healing, it never did take him long to recover. Charlton came over to me and bent down to check on Jimmy, he examined him just like a doctor would and I assumed that's what he must be, for his day job anyway. Very unusual for a shifter, but I guess these were the top level clans of our society, why not be doctors?

"What did you do to them?" He asked while examining Jimmy's eyes.

"Oh, I only put them to sleep. I can wake them up if you need me to?" I explained.

"No, no. No need. I assume they'll wake up when they're ready." He sat back on his knees and looked at me. Really looked at me. It was almost making me squirm under the scrutiny of it. I adjusted myself uncomfortably and started to get myself off the floor. Charlton quickly jumped up to help. I allowed him to help me up as it turned out one of my heels had broken. Pierre was not going to be happy, not to mention that all of Jimmy's clothes lay shredded all over the garden area of the terrace bar. A group from the party were already carrying the other guy back to the house where they were now staying. They decided they preferred it out there by the woods, it had only been her ladyship and a few others that had checked into their intended rooms. The housekeeping team had been called at some point and I got them to take Jimmy back to a free staff room where I figured he could sleep it off. It was strange watching a very large man be lifted of the ground and carried back to the hotel by four small pixies. They were only the height of your average dining table but they were incredibly strong and well built, they also had unbelievably strong magic. That's why they pretty much run this hotel. They took care of everything from severe maintenance issues to general housekeeping. They were notorious clean freaks after all. I think if they had better social skills and weren't so damn grumpy I wouldn't have to come in at all.

Charlton came up beside me and put his jacket over my shoulders, I hadn't realised I was shivering.

"Miss Thomas, I don't know how to apologies enough. Our presence here has been one mess after another and I am deeply sorry for the inconveniences we may have caused." He lowered his gaze to meet mine and he looked honestly hurt.

"Mr Alutiiq, please don't take this the wrong way but right now I couldn't care less. I am exhausted and cold and quiet honestly, pissed! I sincerely appreciate your apologies and maybe we will discuss it further tomorrow once I have decided what is too be done with my idiot brother and whomever that was." I pointed in the direction to which the other man was carried off.

"I cannot thank you enough for being such a gracious host over the last few days, the patience you have shown us is honourable, and I promise to try and keep my clan under control from now on." I gave him a slight nod and the best smile I could manage and left him to the rest of his party and headed back towards the staff quarters.

Chapter Eight

I stood looking over a small meadow. It was filled with wild flowers and edged with tall, old trees. The sun warmed my skin as I lifted my face to Her. It must have been mid to late summer as Her rays were powerful and strong. I could hear a stream running close by and its energy flowed to me, calling to me to join it. From the side I was met with a handful of the softest fur, when I looked down a giant black bear lay next to me in the long grass. It was an unbelievably big black bear, but it didn't frighten me at all. It made me feel safe and happy. I stroked its head and it closed its eyes and groaned happily next to me. As I turned to see if I could see the stream my eyes instead found that the rest of the meadow behind me was full of bears. All different shapes and sizes, there must have been hundreds of them. But as I looked closer the horror of the picture in front of me started to become clear.

Each bear lay with its mate and each set of mates had a cub, but all the cubs were lifeless. They lay still and bloody. The sows appeared to be pinning for their dead cubs and all the boars started to growl the most haunting noises. I felt tears streaming down my face, this was such a tragedy to witness. The bear next to me rose to stand by my side. I reached out to him to feel his fur between my fingers hoping for some kind of comfort from the scene in front of us, he rubbed his shoulder up against me and looked into my eyes, and there they were, my bright amber eyes, glowing at me like gemstones, the warm comforting energy coming from him was incredible and it gave me hope that somehow we could fix the injustice we saw in front of us.

I watched out over the meadow and tried to take in the sorrow that was in front of me. With tears flowing freely down my face as I felt the pain of all the families before us, something squeezed my hand. As I looked down I was now holding a human hand, the thought was overwhelming, and my mouth hung open as I looked at our hands intertwined. Suddenly it occurred to me, his face. I sprung my head up…

And found myself looking up to the ceiling in the staff quarters I was using.

Unbelievable.

I lay there for a time slowly trying to calm myself down, firstly from the devastation I had seen in my dream, all those poor families left destroyed and I had no idea why. And secondly, and more selfishly, from the fact that I didn't get to see his face, that was the closest I had ever come to seeing him, actually seeing him, and I just woke up.

Fricking typical!

"You are not ready," a tiny voice said from the bathroom. Tiny or not it made me nearly jump out of my skin.

"Umm… who is that?" I called out to the bodiless voice.

"It is only me," it replied.

Tired, still a bit sad and pissed off I dragged myself out of bed and went to find whom the voice belonged to. I opened the door to the bathroom and a there, standing on a small stool cleaning the sink was Remelda. One of our housekeeping pixies.

"Hey, Remelda, how're you today?" I asked as I watched her meticulously clean the sink in a room that I only used once in a blue moon.

"Same as I am every day," she replied without breaking her concentration on the sink.

"What did you mean before, Remelda? When you said I wasn't ready. What am I not ready for?" I stood there waiting for her answer but slowly realised she wasn't going to answer me until she finished the sink. Eventually she stepped down from her stool and looked up at me

"Come with me," she said taking me by the hand and leading me into the kitchen area of the room. "Sit," she instructed pointing at a small stall in front of the kitchen sink. I sat and she came and stood in front of me. She rubbed her hands together, seemingly to warm them, and placed them on either side of my temples. I felt her magic instantly and I was being bathed in calmness. She felt like she was looking for something but I had no idea what was going on. After a while she very slowly took her hands away from my face and picked up my hands.

"You are not ready to see the things you cannot see. When you are ready you will know all you wish, and when he is ready for you, he will come for you." I felt her let go of my hands and I took a minute to absorb what she was saying. When my head flooded with questions I opened my eyes but she was gone, I searched the tiny apartment but she was nowhere to be seen, so I made a mental note of the questions I had and stored them for later.

Chapter Nine

I put the night behind me and got myself ready for the day ahead. About a hundred or more of the Ursidae clan were arriving today along with their friends and associates and I needed to be prepared. I checked in on the various offices on my way to the main lobby to check that everything was in full working order and running smoothly. Apart from a few minor maintenance problems from the previous night's antics, all was fine. When I reached my office Jimmy was waiting for me outside looking particularly sheepish.

"Good morning, trouble," I teased as I approached him.

"Evie I am so sorry." He brought me in for a tight hug.

"I bought you along to keep the piece and it turns out you're the one I should have been watching, what were you thinking?" I wasn't particularly mad at him but I couldn't help it. It was too much fun not to make him suffer a little. Plus he deserved it.

"I'm so sorry I had no idea that anyone could be that chivalrous," he said as we went into my office, I sat behind the desk and he collapsed on the couch.

"What are you talking about, chivalrous? What happened?" I asked.

"Well you'd gone to dance with Mr Incredible, so I went to the bar and got talking to some little Genie. Jin. Whatever you call them now, that was making eyes at me. I bought her a drink and we moved over to the railing on the far side of the terrace and was just hanging out."

I raised my eyebrows at him.

"Okay, Okay, I was full on flirting my ass off but she was hot and she's a Genie, man, come on," he pleaded. "Anyway after a bit this big guy walks past and barged into me. I was like: whoa, buddy, am I in the way? And then he started asking if I was supposed to be here with someone else and it wasn't very gentlemanly to be trying to hit on another girl while mine was out of sight. If I'd have known he was being so serious I would never have said what I said next," he said giving me the guiltiest look I have ever seen him produce.

"Do I even want to know what you said?" I asked while dropping my head in my hands.

"I told him it was always more fun when there was the thrill of getting caught..." Jimmy looked genuinely sorry. "I was only messing with the guy but he just lost it and I never got a chance to say I was joking and you were my sister. I swear, I would have never said a word if I had known."

"It's okay, Jim, how could you have known he was a knight of the round table protecting all damsels from unchivalrous cads such as yourself?" We had a good giggle about the whole thing and Jimmy left to go back home and recharge in the sun after last night's activities.

The day went mostly without any hitches or major disasters so an all-round success as far as my staff and I were concerned. I was just finishing up my rounds when Sophia our receptionist brought me a note:

Dear Miss Thomas, if you would kindly join us in the Tennis Bar after 4:30pm

Our planners would like to meet with you about the upcoming festivities.

Yours Sincerely

E Alutiiq

"Who's E Alutiiq?" I asked folding the letter into my trouser pocket.

"No idea, it was just left on the front desk for you," she said already rushing back to reception.

I checked my watch and it was already nearly 6 o'clock, the last thing I needed was another meeting with them but I didn't want to upset them either. I had about an hour before my evening shift as it was Pierre's night off so I decided to quickly get ready before I headed off to meet with them.

I had a quick shower and shoved on a red 1940's style dress with a fishtail finish around the knee. It was one of my favourites actually, it fit exceptionally well and was very flattering, but it was also fun. A lot of my work attire was so boring, all greys and blacks, they were smart and sexy but not like this one, this one had that little something extra, and red was my favourite colour, so win-win! I matched it with some cute red velvet T-bar stilettoes and I was ready to face the music. I decided to wear my hair down this evening, I let my dark auburn waves fall down to the middle of my back and over my shoulders. I pinned a small piece out of my face, had to keep things professional after all. I generally enjoyed the evening shifts as you could get away with dressing up a bit more and it wasn't very often I had any other reason to dress up these days. We also had a formal dining option most nights so you had to look the part whilst on duty.

I stopped by my office to grab all the details I needed about the Alutiiq's upcoming events and headed for the Tennis Bar. Even walking across the patio I could already hear that the night's celebrations had begun and the noise coming from inside the tennis bar was making me regret my decision to meet with them tonight. But this was the job, so I took a deep breath and marched in there.

As soon as I opened the door the level of sounds hit me like a tonne of bricks, and so did the atmosphere. It was thick with testosterone and sex, there were definitely some succubae here and they were definitely enjoying themselves. Mostly people were stood around in groups drinking and talking but there were too many people in there to try and find where I was supposed to be. I decided to make my way to the bar to see if I could get a better view. The bar queue was about ten deep all the way along and even the five trained professionals I had working it were struggling quite a bit. I squeezed in to find my bar manager Steve.

"Do you need some more bodies back here?" I shouted over the noise.

"Wouldn't help," he shouted back. "Not enough room."

And he was right, the tennis bar wasn't big enough to cater for this kind of party, but, as always, I had an idea. For the occasional wedding we had here we had a marque which had its own bar. I managed to get outside and got on the phone to housekeeping. I instructed them to set up for an outdoor wedding outside on the tennis patio minus the marque. I then arranged for some staff from other areas to come and work the bar and offer a waitress service to try keep them seated a bit longer. I also offered to pay them double-time to soften the blow, as they'd probably be working into the early hours.

While I waited for the venue outside to be arranged I helped as best I could behind the bar but within half an hour my exceptional team were done. I opened out the by-folding windows onto the patio and made the announcement about the extension of their party space. I was met with a lot of thanks and praise as most of them made their way outside and it was calmer in no time. They seemed to genuinely appreciate the table service and the atmosphere relaxed instantly, as did my bar staff who looked eternally grateful.

A few seconds into me revelling in my triumph a tiny man came up to me looking very nervous.

"Can I be of any assistance?" I asked him as he nervously twitched in front of me.

"Um… y-yes, Miss Thomas, is it?" he asked and I nodded and smiled in response,

"Um… they would like to speak with you now," he said pointing at a table on the far side of the patio where I could see Charlton smiling broadly and waving at me.

"Oh I see, well thank you very much, I will make my way over shortly." I gave him a curt nod and he scurried off, quite literally.

I gathered up my paperwork that I might need and headed out to the table. I stopped at a few tables on the way to check that everyone was having a good time and to prolong my arrival at theirs. I was not overly keen on learning what it was they actually wanted to discuss.

Walking past one table a large man with dark hair and dark glasses looked up at me as though to say something so I stopped and smiled.

"We'll take three beers, two bourbons and a glass of red for the lady," he said passing me a roll of bills.

"I'm sorry I'm not a waitress but bear with me and I'll…" I looked for the nearest waitress, "Jeannette!" I called across the way and she started to make her way over.

"Do you work here or not?" the man said to me clearly losing his patience.

"I do indeed, Sir, and that is why…" Jeanette arrived "Can you please get me three beers, two bourbons and a glass of red for the lady," I said to her and she jumped to it. "Your drinks will be with you in a moment, Gentlemen. Ma'am," I said with a big smile and went to leave. I had only taken a few steps and the dark haired gentleman called me "Miss?" as I turned he handed me a roll of bills, "you forgot this."

"Oh no need, Sir, on the house," I said and turned to leave.

"I pay for my drinks," he said sounding angry now.

"Sir, you can of course pay for them if you wish but as a gesture I would like you to enjoy them on me," I pulled the biggest smile I could muster and hoped I was looking in his eyes but it was hard to tell through the dark glasses. He didn't responded straight away so I turned to leave at which point a bolt of electricity shot up my arm and sent my paperwork flying. My body was humming with energy and it felt euphoric. I was still for a few moments just enjoying the feeling, but finally pulling myself together I turned to see what it was that was causing it. I found his hand was resting on my elbow where the electricity was generating. The shock hit me cold.

What was he doing to me?

But when I looked up to his face his mouth hung open in what seemed to be shock equal to mine, I stared up at him for some time with my bottom lip tucked between my teeth. I'm not really sure how long we looked at each other but it wasn't until Charlton approached and put his hand on my upper back that I realised he still had hold of me and I was still humming with electricity.

"Ah, Brother, I see you've finally met Miss Thomas," he said looking between the two of us probably trying to work out what had happened, as was I.

"Miss Thomas, my brother. Eli Alutiiq," he said introducing us.

"Um, Evelyn, please," I breathed out, putting my hand out to shake his but it was met with nothing but a blank expression.

"Excuse me," is all he said before bounding off in the other direction and almost taking out one of my waitresses as he passed.

Well that was uncomfortable.

"Please allow me to apologies again for my brother's behaviour, Evelyn. I don't know what's got into him lately." He said following his brother with his eyes as he left the party.

"Not to worry," I said still not really with it and letting my eyes follow him until he was out of sight. "Just one of those things I guess." I had no idea what else to say. "So shall we get on and discuss the plans for the forthcoming events?" I asked, picking up my scattered sheets of paper. Now eager to move on from this peculiar ordeal.

"Oh no, that won't be necessary," he said grinning. "After this here tonight we have complete faith that whatever you have planned for us will be perfect."

Oh goodie, no pressure then.

"Please, you'll join us for a drink though, won't you?" he said offering me his arm.

"Oh, thank you, but maybe later. I'm still on duty and need to tend to a few things beforehand." He seemed disappointed but smiled and made me promise to stop by later.

Chapter Ten

By the time I'd finished doing the rounds and making sure everything and everyone were okay, it was gone midnight. I of course wasn't taking my time doing every little thing I could possible think of just so I wouldn't have to go back to the Alutiiq's and their party.

You keep telling yourself that, Evie.

But by this time it had pretty much taken over the entire resort anyway. Some had moved into the main hotel, some in the garden bar, some on the terrace, and some even out in the woodlands, which could only have been the succubae clans. They loved to party in the woods.

I checked on each little group to make sure all was okay and decided to head out and check the woodlands, they were usually well behaved but checking in wouldn't hurt. I was walking across the resort when I bumped into Charlton walking back to his room.

"Ah, Miss Thomas. I'm so sorry you didn't get a chance to join us. I trust all is well?"

"Good evening, Mr Alutiiq. All is fine I believe. Everyone seems to be having a good time. I hope you've enjoyed your evening?"

"Oh yes, immensely, Miss Thomas, apart from missing the company of a particularly beautiful young manager, it was superb," he said giving me a slightly wicked half grin.

"My apologies, Mr Alutiiq, hopefully another time," I said just to be polite. "I'm just off to check on the party that seems to have moved to the woods, so if you'll excuse me," I said turning to leave.

"Miss Thomas, please allow me to accompany you out there, that's no place for you to be going on your own," he said with true concern etched into his face.

"Thank you, kindly, but the succubae have very little effect on me, I should be fine."

"I'm afraid I'm going to insist on this one, Miss Thomas. This time of year can be surprising to us all and you never know." He offered me his arm and we walked in silence to the path for the woodlands.

I took my normal route as if going to my spot by the stream, just out of habit I suppose. We could only have been a few feet into the trees when the unbelievable atmosphere hit us. The overpowering intoxication they were giving off was challenging to say the least. I felt Charlton stiffen next to me.

"If it's too much I completely understand, you can head back," hoping he would, the last thing I needed was a horny bear tagging along. It was hard enough to focus as it was.

"No, thank you, Miss Thomas, I'll be fine I just needed to adjust. I forget how strong they can be around mating season." He said composing himself and moving us forward. He wasn't as okay as he made out but he seemed to have it under control. After a few minutes along the path he stopped me suddenly. "Do you allow humans on site, Miss Thomas?" he said holding his arm in front of me.

"No, the whole place is warded, no human could get in here without my knowledge. Why?"

"Because, Miss Thomas, there is one out here."

"That's impossible there's no way…" My heart stopped. "Sophia!" I shouted as I broke into a sprint. With panic washing over me I ran as fast as I could. I couldn't let this happen to her. I tried to quiet my brain and let my senses guide me to where she was. I could feel an incredibly strong sexual energy pulling in a certain direction so I followed it until I reached my clearing by the stream. My eyes searched the area frantically in the dark. There she was, completely naked and up against a tree with a succubus between her legs, she was lost in ecstasy and I could feel why, the mojo this guy was putting out was unbelievable, it hit me like a brick wall as I stepped into the clearing.

Luckily I think we arrived before any damage had been done. With a wave of my hand I sent the succubae flying, Sophia groaned in disappointment. By this time Charlton had caught up with me but he didn't look so good. The sex that was floating around was taking its toll on him. I ran to Sophia, she was slumped over against the tree and sobbing uncontrollably.

"Charlton, help me. You have to get Sophia back to the hotel." He was trying so hard but he was losing.

"Charlton focus," I shouted as loud as I could. I dragged Sophia over to him and put her in his arms.

"Charlton Alutiiq listen to me!" I looked him deep into his eyes, "Can you hear me?" he nodded his response trying to hold onto the last bit of his control.

"You have to take Sophia back to the hotel and find the doctor. Do you understand me?" he looked at me for a few seconds and then took off with her in his arms and low rumble growling in his chest, he was using his bear to help him control it.

I spun on my heels and came nearly toe to toe with the succubae. He almost looked like he was stalking me. "Well, well, well..." he took in a long slow sniff and seemed to savour my scent "What do we have here?"

I was frozen on the spot, I felt if I moved I would lose my control. He was pumping me with wave after wave of desire, I could barely stand. He now stood directly in front of me and I could feel his icy breath on my face. His hand came up and slowly moved my hair behind my shoulder. He then placed it on my neck and started to run his fingers along my hairline. I winced with disgust. As much as his enchantment was enticing me it wasn't enough to make me surrender to him.

He lent into me and took a deep sniff of my hair. "Mmm… I see you, my angel. I know what you want." His hand released me and for a second I thought he was letting me go. My eyes popped open in hope, but instead, before me stood a well built, tall, dark haired man completely naked except a pair of dark glasses. I gasped and he smiled. I knew this wasn't real but I could feel it overpowering me. The desire he made me feel was overwhelming me and for some reason now that he looked like Eli Alutiiq I was struggling even more.

The grumpy bear, huh? Who knew?

I instinctively slipped my bottom lip between my teeth and he smiled at me hungrily and slowly lowered his dark glasses. I gasped and almost lost control of my knees. He revealed a set of deep amber eyes glowing like gemstones with a crimson explosion in the centre.

Oh dear!

Before I could be offended by his blatant mishmash of my fantasies he was on me. He had one arm tight around my waist and the other at the base of my neck. His lips crashed into mine. He kissed me deep and slow at first and I let him, it was euphoric. I kissed him back with as much as he gave me. I finally felt I could give into the desires I had unknowingly felt all day for Eli, and most of my life for my amber eyes.

I could feel him start to remove my clothes. He unzipped my dress and it fell to the floor around my ankles his hands went to my rear and groped around greedily.

There was a part of me that knew none of this was real but I had lost all control and was completely lost in his spell.

He pulled me into him tightly and I could feel his growing pleasure big and pulsing against my centre, and it made me ache for more. He moved his hands down to the tops of my thighs and lifted my legs around his waist.

Suddenly my body ignited in a different way, waking me slightly from my trance, like I was coming up for air. My whole body tingled with electricity and fire. It woke me enough to realise what was happening and I started to struggle against him, this just made him hold on tighter.

A roar more frightening than anything I had ever heard unexpectedly erupted from behind me and he dropped me to the floor to protect himself.

I quickly got myself to my feet even though I was still weak and turned to see Eli Alutiiq there with eyes full of crimson and ready to attack. I was stood between the two of them now feeling very confused. I looked backwards and forwards between the two identical men over and over until my brain finally gave in and I stumbled. The real Eli lunged out to catch me before I hit the floor and scooped me up into his arms. I looked into his bright crimson eyes and was only awake long enough for my confused mind to play tricks on me and hallucinate his eyes turning a deep amber with a burst of crimson in the centre, and then I was gone.

Chapter Eleven

My eyes slowly opened and I struggled to focus. The room was bright and cool, the sun was shining on my face, and the warmth of it comforted me.

"Ah, Miss Thomas, it's good to have you back." The voice startled me and I tried to sit up.

"No, no, no. You might be better resting for a while. You had a quiet a night."

I stared at Charlton for a while trying to remember what had happened but it was hazy to say the least. He looked at me and answered as if he knew what I was thinking.

"It might be hazy for a while, my dear. You had a pretty rough night."

I could only remember bits and pieces and couldn't quite decipher between dreams and reality. He gave me a reassuring smile and told me he'd see me down stairs when I was ready. He left the room and gave me a warm but sorrowful smile before closing the door behind him.

I don't know how, but he had arranged for some of my things to be bought to the house as they were laid out on the ottoman at the end of the bed. I felt like I was sporting a rather hefty hangover so I figured a shower would help clear some of the fog. I don't know whose room I was staying in but the bathroom looked like it had been set up just for me, it had all the necessary products a girl could need and there was a toiletry bag with all the washing essentials I could think of.

Weird!

I climbed into the shower and let the perfect pressure wash away some of the heaviness of last night. I was starting to remember a bit more and was met with images of strange men, bears, and oddly, Eli Alutiiq of all people. Still unable to decide what was real I tried to push the uneasy thoughts from my mind as today was a big day. The start of the main Samhain celebrations and that meant no time for distractions, I had to have my head in the game and completely focused.

I started getting ready but as the steam on the mirror started to clear it looked like there was something written there. I couldn't make it out at first but as it became clearer I saw it. My name. Written in the steam on the glass in front of me, in big bold letters was my name. Evelyn Uriel Thomas. Who on earth would write my name in here.

And who would know my middle name to write it?

I stare at it for some time, mainly in shock. As it starts to fade I manage to regain my thoughts and go back to getting ready. Admittedly they were now all over the place and this was the last thing I needed today.

Not having decided what to wear today I head out of the bathroom in my underwear to see what has been sent up for me when I am met head on with a giant chest and shoulders. The impact is accompanied with a surge of energy so strong it sends me flying. I land on the floor with a thud and look up to see Eli Alutiiq looking down at me with a startled look on his face. Quickly realising I'm in my underwear I awkwardly try and get myself off the floor while he stares down at me refusing to look away. Once up, I turn myself around to try and hide myself from him.

Not sure why this is helpful?

I try to look for something to cover myself up. I look over my shoulder at him "I'm sorry to disrupt the show, but do you think you could find me something to cover up?"

He looks as if he regains consciousness and searches for something, finally passing me a dressing gown hanging from one of the wardrobes. He stands side on, not looking at me but not exactly looking away either.

"My apologies, the room was quiet so I assumed you'd left already. I'll give you some privacy."

"It's no problem." I lie. "I didn't realise this was someone's room. Yours I presume?"

"Yes," is all he can seem to muster and then heads for the door. Before I can even ask him about the mirror he's gone.

Once dressed and primped I head down stairs ready to make my apologies and get on with my day. I scan the living areas for someone but there's no one around. Thinking I've got away with having to give awkward thank yous and apologies I beeline for the front door.

"Miss Thomas?" I hear from the kitchen. I cringe, but square my shoulders, plaster on my business smile and head round the corner expecting to see Charlton. Instead I find Eli Alutiiq standing at the stove cooking. The sight stops me in my tracks.

"Sit," he says pointing a spatula at the breakfast bar and not even bothering to look at me. Without hesitation, I sit.

It's getting weird.

"I assumed your schedule wouldn't allow for many breaks today so I wanted to make sure you got something inside you before you set off."

I'm not sure why but there was something about the way he said it that made me squirm.

"Oh, thank you, really. But that won't be necessary. I really should get going." Before I can get off my chair to leave he places a plate of French omelette and side of bacon in front of me and my stomach turned traitor and growled at the smell.

"It's just breakfast, Miss Thomas, it won't hurt you." He turns back to the stove with a half-smile.

I have to admit that it smells amazing and I can't honestly remember the last time I ate, nor was I sure when I would get a chance to eat again. I check my watch and I'm already running behind schedule. But it smells so good and my mouth is watering at the sight of it.

He sits opposite me with a plate of his own with a half smug, half sexy as hell look on his face.

Sexy? That's new.

"It won't bite."

"I'm just not sure I can say the same for the chef."

What am I saying? Did that actually just come out of my mouth?

Sheer embarrassment washes over me and I can feel myself turning a very attractive shade of crimson. He just laughs as I squirm uncomfortably on my stool and turn my concentration to the food. After what seems like an eternity of awkward silence he finishes up his plate and takes it over to the sink, but instead of leaving as I assumed he would he leans on the other counter staring at me. I can feel him studying me, taking me in. It's so incredibly uncomfortable I can't even bring myself to look up at him.

Once I've had my fill of the breakfast, he so strangely prepared for me, I finally look up. He's now stood leaning over the counter writing what looks like a message on a piece of paper. While he's distracted I take this opportunity to get a proper look at him. And he is magnificent. A perfect specimen of a man. Bear. Whatever he is.

He's in a black t-shirt pulled tight over his big arms and even though it isn't fitted you can see he is ripped under there. The t-shirt is accompanied with some loose fitting jeans that make his butt look edible and his un-styled jet black hair falls around his face giving him that ultimate bad boy look. I catch myself almost drooling and quickly try to compose myself before he catches me ogling him.

As he looks up at me I quickly turn away, making myself look incredibly guilty.

"Well thank you so much for breakfast, it was… extraordinary."

Extraordinary? What the… I've gone mad.

I must now be glowing with embarrassment.

He gives me a bemused smile, slips on his sunglasses and makes his way over to my side of the counter. He stands in front me invading far too much personal space and puts his hands on either side of the counter next to me, he angles his head down to meet my ear and breaths "Have a good day, Miss Thomas," and then he's gone. Three giant strides and he's out the door. I'm left in a mess leaning up against to counter, my breathing is hitched, my thighs are clenched and I'm glowing like a beacon of embarrassment.

What the hell was that about?

Chapter Twelve

I try to put the morning and the previous night's events behind me and I let myself get lost in work for the rest of the day. There were a few activities going on during the course of the day and the final guests arriving for Samhain but the main event was this evening. A grand masquerade ball to kick off the festivities in true traditional Samhain style.

For centuries my kind had opened the Samhain festivities with a masquerade ball and I wanted to do it justice. Elegant justice.

We had spent the best part of the day kitting out the banqueting hall in the finest decorations we could conjure; From the vaulted ceilings, lining the walls, hung smooth black and gold velvet curtains all glittering with tiny twinkling lights, the symmetrical staircase and gallery was adorned with glittering black and gold rose garlands that were charmed to give off whatever scent you desired the most, I could smell something sweet and woodsy.

Odd.

The floor was a black tile that looked like tiny gold glittery fireworks erupted underfoot when you walked on it. Pierre enchanted the ceiling to mimic the night's sky, which was a glorious midnight blue that glistened with stars and galaxies alike. The great hall looked the grandest

I had ever seen her and I was humming with anticipation for the evening ahead.

The staff were starting to arrive now and looking fabulous. We had the female staff dressed in thigh length, black and gold, Italian renaissance ball gowns, black stilettoes boots (bewitched for comfort), and elaborate gold masks with black feathers and trim. The men were dressed in elaborately embroidered black velvet waistcoats and dress trousers with gold shirts and black silk cravats. They all looked incredible. Pierre had really outdone himself.

Once they were all briefed on their duties for the evening it was time to get things underway. The bar staff were readying the bar and preparing reception drinks, the waiting staff were setting out their areas and the orchestra had started playing some beautifully gentle mood music. I took a step back to admire our handiwork. It was absolutely beautiful and everything was ready.

"Princess… it's time." Pierre had sought me out as I agreed to let him dress me again this evening and there is nothing he loves more than me giving in to him. I was just finishing up with the order of service for the kitchen staff and we only had about half an hour before the party would be in full swing. Some guests had already arrived, Lady Alutiiq and followers had arrived early so they could formally greet their guests. I secretly had a quick scan of the guests to see if *he* was with them but I couldn't tell with all the costumes and masks.

Pierre finally takes me by the arm and leads me back to the staff quarters so we can start getting ready. We make a quick stop on the way to check on Sophia as she is still healing and unconscious from the night before. Poor child. The doctor assured us she was fine but is keeping her asleep while she recovers as it's a slightly longer process for humans. As much as we wished we could do something we had to trust she was in good hands and of course under permanent guard for security.

Once back in our quarters Pierre starts looking me up and down and circling me like a vulture and its prey. Which I pretty much am this point. After I think the eighth circuit and I'm officially dizzy, he finally stops. Looking more smug than I'd ever seen him, which is no small feat, he claps his hands together and starts laughing. He almost looked like a slightly crazed scientist.

With slight panic setting into my face, and in fear of what he's going to make me wear he finally looks up at me with a heart-warming smile and a tear in his eye. Then, with a very elaborate hand gesture he bows in front of me. "My Queen."

I know his work is done but I'm almost too frightened to look. I know it will be wonderful whatever but the idea of being so elaborate makes me somewhat uncomfortable.

"Close your eyes," he says while slowly turning me towards the mirror. I comply as I don't really want to look at all. Once I achieved a full 180 he stops me. "Look 'ow beautiful you ar', my darling."

I still can't open my eyes.

As I slowly start to open them I am met with so much more than I could have imagined. I'm dressed in a stunning ivory empire line renaissance dress that has a gold bead pattern embellishing the bust area. The entire dress is encrusted with what look like real diamonds that sparkle when they catch the light. It hangs heavy around my feet giving it a beautiful flow on the ground when I move. It also pushes my breast up so high I can almost rest my chin on them. My hair is piled up on top of my head in big luscious curls with a few pieces hanging down around my face and neck. My mask is a pale gold with a mix of ivory beads, sequins and diamonds and is embellished with gold and ivory feathers at my temples leaning back into my hair. I have on long ivory gloves that complement the dress perfectly with their gold and diamond buttons running up the underside. The outfit is beyond stunning and more than I could have hoped for. Pierre is a true genius and I honestly don't know what I would do without him.

Once I'd finished staring at myself in the mirror I turned to thank him and see that he was also done with himself as well. He was adorned in the most elaborate costume I could imagine.

Obviously.

Golds, purples, greens and all mixed in with black velvet trim and a mask that will probably be the most extravagant one this evening.

"Thank you so much, Pierre. How can I ever repay you?"

"Well, a raise wouldn't hurt," he says flicking out his matching hand fan and fluttering his eyelashes at me. We both giggle like a couple of school girls and then we were off.

The ballroom was positively buzzing with energy. It was starting to fill nicely and people looked happy, talking and laughing. The orchestra were playing light, joyful music that accompanied the atmosphere perfectly.

Pierre and I headed to the bar checking on the staff and of course getting ourselves a little tipple to start the evening.

We decided that if we split up to do the rounds it would be done quicker and then we would have more time to enjoy ourselves. He took the left hand side, I took the right and off we went. What felt like two hundred hellos, fourteen rounds of insufferable small talk and a few too many glasses of champagne and the business part of the evening was done. I had schmoozed and entertained about as much as I could handle and now it was time to enjoy myself. Granted I was never really going to be off the clock tonight but it was the official start of Samhain and I needed to let my hair down. Not literally of course, Pierre would kill me.

I headed back to the bar where I'd arranged to meet Pierre and found he'd beat me to it and was chatting elaborately with a tall handsome blonde man in perfect French.

"Good evening, Mr Alutiiq. I trust you are enjoying yourself?" I say with my best all-purpose smile, situating myself next to Pierre, on purpose. I don't know why but seeing him suddenly made me uncomfortable, not sure if it was the memory of the previous night's events or that he reminded me of his brother. But after this morning I wasn't looking to be embarrassing myself any further today.

"Ah, Miss Thomas," he squeals, scooping me up into a very unexpected hug. "I am having a wonderful time, thank you. The place looks superb. I was just telling Pierre here how you have both truly outdone yourselves, I've never seen anything like it. Artists, both of you."

"Well, I would like to share zee credit, but honestly, it was all moi," Pierre said with a wicked smile and exaggerated wink. "Now if you'll both excuse me, I have some, eh, how you say, err, rug to cut," and with another wink he vanished into the crowd.

Still laughing at Pierre's brazenness Charlton suddenly looks at me with a very serious expression. "How are you feeling today, Evelyn? Have you had any after effects from last night?"

Well this turned rather quickly.

"I'm fine, thank you, Charlton." I immediately stiffen at the unwanted reminder of last night's events.

He takes my arm in his hand. "Please, Evelyn, if there is anything at all, you must tell me." The urgency in his voice both startles and panics me.

"Why?" is all I can manage whilst searching his eyes for what he's hiding.

He smiles softly and removes his hand from my arm just as Eli Alutiiq appears next to us.

Just what I need, a tag team.

"Charlton, I thought we agreed that all… formalities, could wait until tomorrow?" he says giving his brother a rather dominating stare.

"Of course they can, Brother, I just thought that if, Miss Thomas remembered anything it might help us to figure out when they might-" Eli cut him off with a raise of his hand. "Enough, Charlie. This can wait, no?"

Charlie?

"Of course. What was I thinking?" Charlton says laughing off the atmosphere that has developed between the three of us and patting me on the shoulder. "Who's for some champagne?" he chortles before heading to the bar and leaving us to deal with the more than awkward vibe now floating around us. It's at this this point I realise that I haven't even looked at Eli since he arrived. And I don't want to either. We both seem to keep our eyes forward and looking out over the crowd as we address each other.

"Are you having a good time?" is all I can muster; I sound more like a blithering fool every time I speak to him.

"Yes, Miss Thomas, the evening you have arranged is more than adequate. On behalf of my family and myself, we thank you greatly."

Well that was ceremonial.

"Will you be dancing this evening?" he says looking in the opposite direction.

He is so odd. He's starting to give me whiplash.

"Um… yes, I suppose I will be. Will you?" I ask beyond awkwardly, not really knowing how to act around him at all. He seems to make all of my smarts fly right out of my head.

"Very good, well then hopefully I will see you out there." He gives me a curt nob and walks away into the crowd.

He's sooo weird!

I stand there for some time staring at the part of the crowd he vanished into just trying to make some sense out of his behaviour. It's not totally inappropriate but he gives off the strangest vibes. And I can't seem to get a grip when he's around.

Not to mention he's a complete ass.

Trying to shake the aftermath that is Eli Alutiiq, I knock back what's left of my champagne and head for the dance floor. By this time the party is in full swing and I join just in time to partake in one of our traditional Samhain dances; The Corofin Plain. Granted the music was slightly more sophisticated than it was thousands of years ago but it usually still had a good Irish beat to it and definitely got everyone on their feet. I joined Pierre and the group he was dancing with, six of us in total and the other groups formed around the dance floor. By the way the dance floor felt I think everyone was either dancing or watching as the atmosphere was electric. Once the intro kicked in everyone sprang to life and the dance began.

It was a cross between and old fashioned ballroom set dance and an Irish Jig. We leapt around the floor at full speed, paired up, swapping partners, dosy-dow'ing and spinning. With every joyous step the dancefloor burst to life, letting off tiny multi-coloured fireworks underfoot. Amazing really, how so many people of all ages, from such different walks of life, all know the same dance. But this was the beauty of Samhain, it didn't matter who you were, all that matters is now.

I was flung around the dance floor till I felt sick and laughed so hard I could barely hold myself up, but I definitely wasn't alone, most of the congregation looked the same. The dance was just starting to slow down and we were on our last few turns around the room when I saw them, like beacons calling out to me. The brightest amber eyes I had ever seen, blazing through a black mask, burning into me like I was the only one in the room. They froze me where I stood. As the rest of the dance carried on around me all I could do was get lost staring at my amber eyes, part of my brain wasn't even sure if I was hallucinating or even awake. Everyone finally came to stop around me and thankfully only those closest to me seemed to notice my odd behaviour. Not that I really noticed them. I was lost.

Eventually too many people were moving in our eye-line and it was getting harder to stay focused on them. In the end I had to look away so I could get out of the way for the next dance to start. I immediately started in the direction they had been in but was unable to find them again. I looked frantically for some time but they had moved on and I had lost them again. If nothing else, providing I was in fact awake and not hallucination, they were here, in this crowd, at this party, and they saw me too. There was no way of denying it, they looked at me the way I looked at them. With longing, lust and not forgetting mild confusion. Annoyingly I couldn't tear myself away from his gaze long enough to get a look at what he was wearing or any other feature for that matter, other than his mask was black, and a black mask in this room pretty much narrowed it down to half the guest list.

I calmed my search to something a lot less manic and by this time I could see Pierre stalking me from the other side of the room flanked by two strapping young men and a bottle of champagne. This was the part of any social event that I detested, the one where my friends and family would take the upmost pleasure into trying to set me up with some poor young man who in no way stood a chance, not because they weren't good enough, just because they weren't... well... him.

Chapter Thirteen

After Pierre introduced his two new friends, and gave me a more than embarrassing introduction, he led us all to a table where we sat for some time just talking and drinking. The older of the two men seemed most interested in me, engaging me in conversation and practically hanging on my every word, but the younger of the two gave off an unusual vibe. He didn't speak to me, not even once, but seemed to spend most of his time watching me, as if he was studying me, taking me in. At first I didn't really pay much attention to it but after some time it started to unnerve me. He seemed too interested for someone who wasn't even engaging me in conversation.

The longer we sat, the more we drank, and the drunker I got. After what must have been several bottles of champagne I was definitely feeling the effects and so was everyone else in the ballroom. The whole room was alive with energy and so was I. I had felt like I'd been polite enough with my current guests and it was time to move on and I only seemed to have one place in mind, Eli Alutiiq. Not really sure why or what I planned to do once I found him but he was all I could think about in my intoxicated state.

Once I made my excuses and said my goodbyes to my present company I was off. Into the crowd of drunken masses I went, but I found the further I got the harder it became for me to walk straight, I knew I was drunk but I had no idea I'd reached the levels off inappropriateness. I suddenly felt like the room was watching me and my embarrassment took over. I looked for the nearest exit and convinced myself that all I needed was some fresh air.

Once outside on the terrace I found a secluded bench and slumped myself down on it. My head was spinning and everything was becoming hazy. I felt as though I was heavily drunk but somewhere in my mind I was untouched by the effects. I could feel my body losing control but there was nothing I could do to stop it. I let my head lean back on the bench and suddenly realised someone was sitting next to me, I hadn't even realised they'd approached. I willed my body to look at them but I couldn't move. I felt a hand brush my cheek and slide a stray strand of hair behind my ear. I then felt the breath on my neck where light kisses were being placed up and down it, and all I could do was sit there. I had no power to even look at who was next to me let alone stop them. I felt a slight spark ignite somewhere inside of me, my powers springing to life but at the same time a hand came down on each of my cheeks I could feel myself being filled with warmth, love, ecstasy, passion, and wild lust. I think a part of me knew what was happening but I didn't have the strength or desire at that point to fight it. I let the euphoria wash over me and I enjoyed every wave of it.

After some time, could have been seconds, minutes, who knows? I felt myself being carried. I was in someone's arms. I had no idea where I was going and my body was still unresponsive, I just let myself lay there and enjoy the perfect, sexy, peace I was being bathed in. Eventually we came to a stop and I was put on the ground, I could feel hard bumpy earth underneath me and I could smell the all too familiar smell, and hear the familiar noise of my stream. We were at my spot.

Who on earth would bring me here?

I could hear someone now, a stranger's voice gently chanting in the background. I had no idea what they were saying, I didn't even recognise the dialect, but I could recognise a spell in any language. I lay there motionless, unable to move, with no control over any part of my body and only conscious in the back of my mind, knowing what was about to happen, knowing that I had no way out of it.

A part of me longed for the conscious part of me to shut down as well, at least if this was inevitable, if it had to happen, don't let me be aware of it, don't let me lie here and watch this happen. Nobody deserved that.

Silence fell after a few minutes and I felt a body join me on the floor. They started by moving all my hair out of my face and pushing it back behind my ears. Then I felt them smelling my neck, taking in deep, greedy breaths. Inhaling my power and using it to fuel their drive.

"I see you, my angel, I know what you want," he said burying his face into my chest and positioning his body above mine.

I could have opened my eyes at this point to confirm who it was but I didn't need to. I knew it was the succubae from the night before, and I didn't want to give him the satisfaction of seeing the tears pooling in my eyes. He had come back to finish what he had started and all I could do was lie there on the cold hard ground and let him. I had to assume that he had slipped me something during the ball.

He lowered his body onto mine and his hand quickly found its way up my dress, he moved slowly but purposefully, his hand gripped my ass and squeezed it as he groaned in pleasure. His other hand went to the back of my head and lifted it to his so he could continue to inhale me as he groped me under my dress. He slowly found his way to my underwear and ran a finger along the seam, tracing the outline of them all the way to the apex of my thighs and then back up to my stomach. He took one last deep breath and then his body was gone, he wasn't on top of me anymore and in some mad fit of hope I flung my eyes open to see what had caused this glorious separation.

"Well there you are, my angel," he said standing over me grinning with pleasure and undressing himself. "I'm so glad you decided to join the party."

All I could do was meet his stare, I didn't even have to power to show my despise for him through my eyes.

"Don't worry, my little light, I'll give you what your dirty little mind desires. What it craves."

Suddenly my head filled with fog and couldn't focus on anything, I felt like I was spinning out of control and couldn't catch my breath when I suddenly smacked into something hard.

"Woah there, take it easy, I've got you. Calm down. He's gone, he's gone."

I look up and see Eli Alutiiq holding me to his chest, taking my weight and the succubae lying on the ground a few feet away. I can't help myself, still full of all the dread and lust from before I burst into tears, it's a full release of emotion and panic and my body almost fits with relief. After a few minutes I regain some composure and remember I'm still being held up by Eli.

"I'm so sorry, I couldn't stop him, I didn't know what to do I just…."

"Shhhh, it's okay now. You don't have to worry about a thing," he says as he scoops me into a hug so strong I feel like he's trying to put my broken pieces back together.

"Thank you," is all I can muster as I wrap my arms around him in return.

The hug goes for longer than is deemed appropriate but it feels necessary, it feels right. As I slowly start to release my arms he sets me on my feet, but when I look up at him his eyes are closed. He looks almost pained and like a reflex my hand is on his face. I don't know what's causing him such pain but I need to fix it.

Please let me be the one to fix it.

He instinctively leans his face into the palm of my hand and inhales me. This time it feels exquisite. It's such an intimate act between Mystics and is only usually done between couples as it's an exchange of power, but I feel like I would let him breathe me all day, except it would probably kill me. But in this moment it feels like magic, pure and simple. I notice his hands tighten round my waist slightly but he almost seems unsure about it. I can't wait for him to decide so I do it for him. I slowly bring my other hand up to his face and gently pull him towards me. Once we're nose to nose I lean up on my tiptoes and plant a soft kiss on his lips. He doesn't respond at first and I search his face to see if I've completely misread the signal but then a half smile turns up the corner of his mouth as he presses his body against mine and kisses me. The kiss starts off smooth and firm but quickly turns into a hungry scurry from both of us. I can feel his need and desire and it only fuels my own. I lock my arms around his neck and he lifts me off my feet with one arm around my back and one hand gripping my behind. I hitch my dress as he lifts me up and I wrap my legs around his waist, our kiss deepens. My hands are in his hair gripping chunks of it and pulling slightly and his hands hungrily grope my body shooting warmth and desire straight to my core. My hands start to move down eager to feel his tort physique under my skin and I start to pull his top over his head. He sets me on my feet and I realise my back is against a tree and I'm able to use it for support, I lean back into it and look over his beautiful chest glistening at me in the moonlight. He brushes a strand of loose hair behind my ear and cups the back of my head. He turns a handful of my hair in his fist and pulls into him roughly, its startles me slightly but before I think on it he is kissing me again pulling me into his body. He makes quick work of getting me out of my dress and underwear. I'm now completely naked and he takes a step back to look at me. I steady myself against tree again and try to clear my head.

What am I doing?

As much as I apparently want this man, can I really just give myself to him like this in the woods? Before I can talk myself out of it he's on his knees in front of me now also naked and planting small kisses on my stomach and slowly parting my thighs with his hands. Just as his kisses start to descend towards my core I hear something. I can't quite put my finger on what it is but I feel like it wakes me up a little bit.

"What was that?" I ask putting my hands on his shoulders to try and stop him.

"Shhh, my angel, it was nothing. Just be here with me." He doesn't stop his descent and now I start to panic. I can hear noises getting closer, louder and he called me 'my angel' which sets off alarm bells but I can't put my finger on why, my head starts to get foggy and I can't concentrate. The noises are getting closer and he's getting more eager, almost aggressive.

In the back of my mind I can hear people shouting, familiar voices calling out to me but I can't work out where they are. I look around me frantically trying to find the source but no one is around. In my panic and confusion, I try to push him away from me but he only grips me tighter and seems angered now.

"Stop please, I don't understand." A searing pain runs through my brain, something is fighting against me but I can't seem to think straight. Nothing makes sense.

He grabs me furiously and turns me around pushing me up against the tree, my face is pressed up against dark rough bark and he's pressed up against me. I can feel him trying to enter me when the ground under us starts to shake. He falls backwards away from me and I cling to the tree just to stay on my feet. He appears to be being dragged across the clearing by an invisible force and all I can do is think about the fogginess in my head and how much everything hurts. I feel my body getting weaker and weaker as I start to slip in and out of consciousness.

Then I can hear him, the real him. "Evelyn, I need you to wake up now. I need you to hear my voice and come back to me. Can you hear me, Evelyn? I need you to come back to me."

I force my mind to concentrate on his voice, only his voice. I let it consume me, let it guide me back to reality. And suddenly there I am.

I'm lying on the ground in my clearing, wrapped in a blanket being cradled by Pierre. I look up at him in complete surprise, he wasn't who I expected to see and I can't help the disappointment that washes over my face.

He looks down at me with the softest expression I've ever seen on him and places a feather-weight kiss on my forehead, brings me into him and just holds me. I'm pretty sure he's crying but I'm not totally sure what's going on anymore. My brain is foggy as hell and I feel like I've just gone ten rounds with Mike Tyson. But I let him hold me in silence as I try to make sense of the scene around us. There are a group of men scattered around with one of them giving orders about where they should be going and another group off the way a bit, getting dressed. If all wasn't strange enough Charlton comes marching over to us in what appears to be a pair of boxer shorts and kneels down in front of me.

"Sorry, Pierre, I need to check her vitals." he leans over me as Pierre loosens his grip, he checks my pulse against Pierre's watch he then moves on to look in my eyes and then rests his hand on my forehead, presumably taking my temperature.

"All seems fine overall. Evelyn, do you remember anything at all?" he says giving a very stern look but trying to soften it at the same time.

All I can do is stare at him.

I have no idea how to answer the question.

I have no idea what I remember and what I do seem to remember I can't make any sense of. So I just stare at him.

He suddenly takes my hand in his, startling me with the unexpectedness of it, and wraps his other hand over the top. "I will never be able to apologise to you enough for allowing this to happen to you again. I honestly thought we'd have more time and I would be able to prepare you for… anyhow, please rest assured that we will do everything in our power to make sure he pays for his actions and I promise you his punishment will be just," and with a nod of his head he leaves.

Still sat in Pierre's arms I look out, dumbfounded at the scene in front of me, still lost in foggy confusion and the only thing I can think to do is sleep. My eyelids are beyond heavy and my body is screaming for me to let sleep take me. I lean back into Pierre and close my eyes.

Within seconds I'm scooped up into giant arms and I can feel his warmth running through me and the unmistakable electricity that surges between us when we touch.

"I've got you, my Little Witch. Rest now." And I do. I let myself sink into his giant warm chest and drift away into dark peace.

Chapter Fourteen

I wake up with a start. My head still full of dreams of bears, succubae and Maker knows what else.

Again. Yay!

I ache from head to toe and my brain feels like it might be trying to pound its way through my skull.

I look around trying to see where I am, it's still dark out and the only light is coming from a crack in the door of the landing outside. I'm in the house, in Eli's room. For some reason this makes my stomach flutter. I don't remember much from last night but I do remember him. The him that wasn't really *him*, and the him that was. I remember him carrying me here. He must have put me to bed, and someone at some point had also put me in what feels like a man's shirt.

Please be his.

Although my mild infatuation, borderline obsession, with him was somewhat unwarranted as we've only spoken a handful of times, for most of which he was highly unpleasant and always completely unreadable, I couldn't help it. I was unexplainably drawn to him. Annoyingly so.

After spending a few moments getting lost in my thoughts, thinking about my growing infatuation I suddenly feel like I'm not alone. I was so busy day dreaming about tall, dark, and ridiculously handsome bear-men that I forgot to actually scan the room. I felt the bed next to me move slightly and before I could think I shot to the other side of the room in a defensive stance, my eyes darting around looking for who to attack.

Pretty sure I've never moved so fast.

"Sorry, I didn't mean to startle you. Thought it would be best to give you a minute to wake up... but I guess not." He must have been sleeping as his voice had reached a whole new level of sexy gruffness.

Awash with shear embarrassment I quickly compose myself and adjust my nightshirt to make sure I'm relatively descent.

"Please, I didn't mean to make you uncomfortable," he said getting of the bed "I just wanted someone to be here in case you needed anything. I didn't want you to wake up alone."

As he gets of the bed and heads for the door I scurry over and jump under the covers in a hope to cover my shame. Although it's possibly a little late for that, considering last night he carried me here completely naked and wrapped in a blanket after being found with some crazed succubae face deep in my undercarriage.

The thought makes me shudder and I shake my head to try and clear it from my mind. Which seems to be handling all this pretty well, I might add.

He lingers for a beat and then turns to leave.

"Stay," is all I can manage to blurt out. I didn't realise how dry and sore my throat was. I grab my throat feeling like I'm about to choke when he's there next to me holding out a glass of water. I drink it down in one and clear my throat. "Thank you... Will you… Stay? With me? For a while?" I can't even look up at him while I sheepishly blurt out random request, but I so want him to stay.

Without a word he gets up and heads for the bathroom. I hear the tap running for a while and when he returns he's changed into a pair of low hanging slacks.

Be still my beating heart.

He walks round to the other side of the bed and makes himself comfortable on top of the covers.

We both sit in the awkward silence for some time and I am feeling beyond uncomfortable with his proximity. I'm not looking but I know his chest is exposed and all I can think about is curling up to him and resting my head on it. I find my eyes looking everywhere but in his direction and I know I should lay down and try and get some rest but my body doesn't want to comply, it's stuck, almost glued in the spot and is refusing to move.

"Are you not tired? I thought you'd be exhausted." I can feel his eyes on the back of my head and I know I should turn to look at him but something stops me, something is telling me I'm not ready.

Ready for what?

"Yeah... I think maybe a bit too exhausted. I feel a bit wired, you know? Like I need to run a mile and sleep for a week all at the same time."

"We can go for a run, if that's what you need."

"Because I need you to see me run? No thanks." It's out of my mouth before I can stop it.

"And why would me seeing you run be a problem?" I can hear the smug smile in his voice and I know I'm blushing a deep shade of crimson, and I'm oh so thankful that's it too dark for him to see my face.

I sit, still looking away from him, genuinely pondering his question. Why would it be a problem? Why does he affect me the way he does? I'm not sure I even like this man and I certainly don't know him. So why such a pull, why do I care what he thinks of me, why do I care if he likes me, if he desires me, if he sees me as an equal? The more I think about it the more I realise how much of an affect he has on me. Too much!

I'm in trouble!

Once I've finally finished berating myself about my feelings for the Adonis lying next to me, and that's what I've decided they are, *feelings*, I eventually turn to look at him. Much to my liking his eyes are closed and he appears to be asleep. Eli Alutiiq, the most beautiful creature I've ever laid my eyes on is lying in bed next to me and I've allowed him to go to sleep.

What an idiot!

I stare at him for a while, taking him in. Closely examining every inch of him, the inches that I can see in the restricted lighting anyway. And he is glorious. His bronze skin is perfectly smooth and pulled tight over his muscles, jet black hair forms a perfectly small triangle shaped patch on his chest and his silky soft hair frames his face beautifully, making me want to lean over and brush it back behind his ear. He is wickedly handsome. He has full plump lips that frame his brilliantly white teeth and a chiselled square jaw that he apparently grinds when he's asleep. A slightly crooked nose, that's big, but nothing near offensive, and his eyes, it suddenly occurs to me I don't know what colour his eyes are. I've never actually seen him up close without sun glasses or when he's not in a rage. I know they're a terrifying shade of red when he's in bear form or extremely pissed, but no idea what they're like normally. I would guess, like his brother, Charlton's, but then Charlton is much lighter than his brother is, his hair is blonde and his features are much, much lighter.

An image of my amber eyes at the dance earlier quickly flashes across my memory, but it's gone as soon as it has come. I push thoughts of this evening out of my mind and I eventually agree with myself that tomorrow I will find out, after all, there's no point trying to fantasise about a man if you don't have the complete image.

I finally lay myself on the bed next to him, getting as close as possible without touching him, and quietly imagining what it would be like to fall asleep wrapped in his giant arms. Just as I feel sleep is coming for me he leans over and wraps an arm around me, pulling me into him. He tucks one arm under my head and the other wraps around my waist. At first I'm frozen stiff, but his warmth and my extreme tiredness make it too difficult not to relax. I let out a deep sigh and sink into his embrace, feeling his large chest breathing into my back. I let the perfect feeling consume me and let sleep take me somewhere peaceful.

Chapter Fifteen

The sun is blindingly beautiful and rising over a rocky
shoreline. I sit on a large boulder rocking a tiny bear cub in my
arms. He isn't moving, he's cold and limp. I look down at him
and my heart cries. I can feel the pain his mother must have felt
when she was told he wasn't breathing as if he were my own. I
mourn for the little one in my arms, willing him to wake up, to
move, breath, show me any sign of life at all. But he just lays
there, limp and still.

As I look up from the tiny bundle in my arms I am
surrounded by bears. Some big, some small, some giant, but all
looking at me longingly. One of them approaches the boulder I
am sat on and bows before me, I can see the smile in his eyes.
"Thank you," he says looking down at the now baby boy in my
arms, who is now looking up at me and smiling. My heart swells
with joy and pride. I can't believe it, is this not the bear cub that
was just limp and lifeless? I look around the many faces in front
of me for answers stopping at a warm pair of eyes looking up at
me from the crowd. It's one of the smaller bears, a female I
believe, her eyes are glistening with tears. She approaches me
and joins the larger bear in front of me and bows.

"Our Saviour! Our Lifeline! Our Queen!" roars the giant
bear in front of me. The entire congregation then tilts back onto
their hind legs and roar out their cheers and thanks.

I look down at the beautiful squirming bundle of beauty in
my arms and stare into his beautiful eyes, his beautiful deep

amber eyes glistening like gemstones with a burst of crimson in the centre. I know this boy… He is from my flesh… He is mine… and he is ours.

I wake up still staring at the same eyes.

It takes me a while to focus in on them but they're definitely there, staring back at me. Deep amber gemstones with a burst of crimson in the centre, soothing me deep within. I have no idea how long I stare at them, but I am lost, my brain running wild, trying to figure if I'm still asleep, trying to make sense of what it is I'm looking at. When my brain finally calms down I can take in the whole picture. I'm still lying in bed, looking up at Eli and he is looking down at me with a now very confused and slightly startled impression. "Are you okay?"

All I can do is stare up at him. I can't move, speak, or even compose my thoughts, I just stare back at him like a dear in headlights.

"Evelyn, are you okay?" he moves his hand up towards my face and my body goes into panic. Before I can think a cramping feeling pulls at my gut and the next thing I know I'm standing in the middle of the living room at my parents' home. My dad looks startled to say the least, he just looks up at me blinking; the cookie he must have just dunked in his tea dripping onto his belly.

"Evie, pet… what the Maker…?" he can't seem to finish the question, probably because he's not sure what to ask.

"Sorry, Dad." Is all I can muster and I dart out of the room and out into the back yard. It's absolutely hammering it down with rain but I need to be outside, I need to be somewhere I can focus and try to collect my thoughts. My brain is still awash with half memories and dreams and is struggling to decipher which is which. I pound through our back yard in seconds and hit the edge of the forest that lines it. Once I'm in the cover of the trees I start searching for my clearing. Like at the lodge I have a Thomas Spot at home as well. Although it's on a much bigger scale. It normally takes me about ten minutes to get there from the houses but today I've done it in record time. I reach the edge of the forest and it opens onto a clearing and then a river, this one is no trickling stream though, it's a huge vast body of water and looks like it would be perfect for white water rafting, it's fast, and furious, and home to some impressive sarsens, also known as druid stones which are very uncommon in this part of the world. They call to me like old friends.

I stand at the edge of the river for a moment and take in the view. No matter what mood you're in, you shouldn't take a view like this one for granted. Giant trees of all different species line the edge of the river on both sides, and the fierce waters smash against giant boulders as it courses its way down to a waterfall, leaving behind a heavenly looking white mist in its wake. It's truly breath-taking.

I take my first steps into the water and let my feet sink into the bed slightly. I close my eyes and let it start to work its magic. I stand perfectly still for at least a few minutes and try to clear my mind of everything that wants to bombard it, but it's no use, it's too noisy in there, I need to go deeper. I slip off the shirt I'm still wearing from the night before and my underwear and leave them on the bank behind me.

No point getting them wet.

I make my way further into the river. The current is strong and powerful but I trust it, it wants to heal me, not hurt me and I can feel that. I feel it start to cleanse my thoughts the deeper I go. I'm sure if anyone could see me they'd think I was committing suicide just strolling into the rapids like this, but it's what I need and I know it will keep me safe.

I keep going until the water just covers my chest, I steady my feet and again let them sink into the bed. I close my eyes, submerge my head for a few seconds, and that's enough. With my body completely submerged I can feel my magic take over, I can feel the process beginning. I flick my head out of the water, my eyes closed. I feel the water swirl around me, changing its direction, this way and that, mimicking my thoughts trying to find some control, a steady path in the madness. Then it comes, the calm. It feels as if the water enters my veins and calms me from within. It centres my magic and I feel it flow through me with force, focus and determination.

But this time something feels different, it feels more controlled more enabled. I let it consume me like never before, I feel it fill every inch of my being in an almost savage and primal manner. Suddenly something's different, I'm not in the river anymore. I can no longer feel the water flowing past me. I open my eyes and can't believe what I'm seeing. The water is swirling in the air around me and I have risen a few feet above where the surface should be. I can feel the water waiting for my instruction, it is ready to obey me, I only have to ask.

I slowly move my hands in circular motions and the water mirrors my actions. It spirals around itself making little whirlpools in its wake.

I close my eyes and try to concentrate on everything that has happened over the last few days, trying to piece together all that I've seen.

Images of bears, succubae, amber and crimson eyes flash through my memory with aggression and I can feel the water around me responding. I try to calm myself and regain control but I can't seem to stop the images from forming. I feel as though the water has gained control of my thoughts and is deciphering them for me.

It sends flashing images coursing through my mind's eye until it finds what it's looking for. And suddenly there he stands, in all this glory. His perfect form, glossy black hair, beaming smile and deep amber eyes, glistening like gemstones with a burst of crimson in the centre, are staring back at me. My body suddenly reacts. I can feel myself convulsing but I have no control over anything. I feel the water start to flow around me wrapping me in a whirlpool of my thoughts and desires. I am out of control and so is the river I have disrupted. I don't know how to deal with the mess my thoughts are creating and it lifts me higher and higher into the air.

The water still wrapping itself around me carries me higher still and then suddenly calm. A single moment of calm washes over me when I realise I've found him. My amber eyes are real and they belong to most beautiful creature I'd ever seen. In my clarity I suddenly feel the water around me fall away, but then I feel myself falling.

I'm hurtling back to the surface of the river at a terrifying speed. I cover my face with my arms and just as I'm about to hit the surface I stop. I tentatively open my eyes and see the water has caught me again and is holding me gently above its surface. Just as my body relaxes a flickering thought of Eli pops into my head and the water hurtles me back up into the air and wraps me once more in a giant whirlpool, this time carrying me towards the edge of the waterfall further downstream. In a panic I try to turn myself around but just seem to make things worse, and I'm now moving faster.

Now approaching the edge of the waterfall I try to prepare for what's to come. I instinctively take a deep breath and close my eyes when suddenly I am lifted into the air and everything becomes calm. Stillness. I open my eyes to see the water is gently carrying me slowly over the edge of the fall and now seems to be caressing me, helping me, soothing me. I let the water finish its decent and it sets me down gently. I land safely on the bank about 3 miles down the river from where I had started, I looked back at the now calm river flowing as normal, almost in disbelief of what had just happened, how was it even possible? I'd seen some people do some pretty weird stuff in my time but this was something else. Slightly staggered about what had just happened I gathered my naked self and made my way back to my clothes.

Chapter Sixteen

I decided it would be in my best interest to stay home tonight and let Pierre deal with the aftermath of yesterday. I knew I should go in but I needed time to get my head around things. My folks were throwing their annual Samhain build-up party and I figured it would be a good way to take my mind of things.

Sure!

Around nine o'clock people started to arrive, I was still in my room debating whether or not to get changed or just stay in my sweats when my dad knocked on the door. "Hey, Kiddo, mind if I come in?"

I just nodded and shifted on the bed so he could sit next to me. He sat heavily on the bed and shifted so he could face me.

"How you doing, Kiddo?"

"Yeah…. I'm fine, Dad"

"Okay, so are we gonna talk about what happened earlier? Or shall we just pretend you didn't catch me eating that cookie?"

He always knew how to make me laugh.

"Seriously, Kiddo, should we be talking about what happened earlier? 'Coz I don't know about you, but I don't get a lot of people just appearing in my living room every day?"

"Dad, I just… I don't know what happened. I honestly have no idea what is going on right now. One day my life is just coasting along as normal and the next, I don't know my ass from my elbow."

"So why don't you tell old dad what the problem is, maybe I can help?"

So, I did. I explained, probably in way too much detail, about what had happened over the last few days while my dad listened intently, and without a word he just stood up and left my room. I assumed I had shared too much and he needed a minute but he then came back into the room with a box, he placed it down in front of me on the bed and gave a sheepish grin.

"What's this?" But as I looked at it I felt like I already knew what it was.

"It's yours," he says. "But it came with strict instructions not to give it to you until it was time, and well… I think it's time, Kiddo."

I ran my fingers over the markings on the lid like I knew them, even though I had no idea what they meant and I didn't understand the dialect at all. I don't think I'd ever even seen it before either. It was beautiful though, it seemed to sing to me, like a gentle humming as I ran my fingers over them. "Time for what? What did you have to wait for?"

"I think it best you open it when you feel ready to, and see what it has to say for itself," and with that he kissed me on the head and left the room.

I stared at the box for some time, just running my fingers over the engravings deciding whether now was the right time to open it or not. When I finally decided it was probably a bad time as I had no idea what it would hold and we had a yard full of people downstairs I slid it under my bed and decided to join the party.

It was now pushing midnight and the party, for the most part, was in full swing. My mum was playing honkytonk on the piano. Her go to party move. My dad was starting the bonfire in the pit he made in the middle of the yard and my brothers and sisters were all rather inappropriately engrossed in whomever they'd picked to be their fun for the evening. Except Anna-May, of course, she was over by the edge of the forest that bordered the yard seemingly performing her own idea of a Samhain ritual. Probably involved howling at the moon or such like, she did love a good archaic ritual. Then I felt it, as I moved out onto the decking I felt the pulse of electricity whenever he was near me. I held onto the railing of the porch for support as I desperately searched the crowds for him.

So, this morning you're teleporting out of his arms in a blind panic and now you're desperate to see him… okay, Evie, get a grip, girl.

Then there it was, the crackle of electricity, the heat at my back.

"Looking for someone?" he was right behind me and his voice was deep and gravelly, and oh so intoxicating. I was frozen to the spot but my body was alight with energy. All I wanted to do was turn around and throw myself at him but something was stopping me, and I felt like that something was him.

I took in a deep shaking breath to try and calm myself. It didn't work. My whole body could feel him, every inch of me was aware of his presence, every sense heightened. I wanted to turn and face him but he was stopping me. "Why won't you let me turn around?"

"Great party, it was very nice of your father to invite me in."

"Don't change the subject. Why won't you let me turn around?"

"I don't know what you're talking about."

"Don't play games with me, why won't you let me turn…" before I could finish the sentence he was against my back, I could feel his breath in my ear.

"Because, Miss Thomas, the last time we were face to face you disappeared into thin air and it took me all day to find you, I'd rather not have a repeat performance, if it's all the same to you."

His arms were either side of mine and our bodies were humming with electricity. I knew he could feel it, it was so powerful. I almost felt others would feel it if they came close enough. "So how did you find me?"

"I tracked you."

"You tracked me? What the hell does that mean?"

"I'm a bear," he said as if it answered the question.

"You're a Bear?"

"Yes, you know this."

"Yes, but I don't see how that explains how you found me?" I was slowly remembering how odd this all was, every time we interacted he annoyed me immensely and always came off as such an arrogant jerk.

"Look, how I found you is irrelevant. All that matters is that you're safe." He said shortly.

Feeling that whiplash again.

"Well, thank you for checking on me, but if that's all you came here for then I'm fine," I said with a huff and folding my arms trying to make more space between us.

It didn't work.

He leant in closer to me so I could feel his breath on my neck. "You seem disappointed, Miss Thomas, what else would I have come here for?" I could hear the smile in his voice but it didn't stop me from turning pure crimson. I so wanted to be able to walk off and busy myself in the crowd but he kept me locked on the spot.

Maker he felt good.

He hesitated for a few seconds and eventually took a few steps back allowing me to move. I appreciated the freedom but missed his body more. I allowed myself a moment, pretending it would prepare me for turning around, but who was I kidding. I almost didn't want to. I wasn't sure I was prepared to see them again, on a real person, a person that I wasn't sure I even liked. Or worse, I wasn't sure I was prepared to not see them.

I slowly turned myself around and found myself staring at his shoes. I just couldn't bring myself to look up.

"Are you just going to stare at my feet?"

I shut my eyes and took a deep breath, but I just couldn't do it, it felt too overwhelming. It was too big a moment to just simply brush by. I had waited forever to see these eyes in the flesh and now that I was about to, I wasn't sure that could handle it. What if it was a repeat of this morning? What if I just disappeared again? What if they weren't there? I couldn't do it and I could feel myself start to panic, my breathing became laboured and I went turn away again.

"Oh no you don't," he said as he grabbed my arms, stopping me from turning away. "Miss Thomas, open your eyes." He lifted a hand to my cheek, brushing it gently he then ran his hand under my hair and around my neck, my skin was ablaze with his touch, it was exquisite. I opened my eyes and stared down at his chest.

"Miss Thomas… Evelyn… please?" His voice sounded pained and I was so compelled to see if the pain reached his face I looked up and straight into his eyes.

There they were, the deepest amber, like the most beautiful gemstone I'd ever seen with a burst of crimson in the centre. I searched them as he did mine. I don't really know what I was looking for, but I do know that I found it.

"I can't believe I found you," he said as he looked at me in amazement.

"Found me? What do you mean?"

"Evelyn, I've waited a lifetime, several lifetimes in fact, to find you. I can't believe you're real." He said through a half laugh half cry.

"Several lifetimes? What do you mean?" I couldn't believe what he was saying, could it be possible that he too has been seeing me every night like I have him.

"I've been looking for you for over 200 years, Evelyn Thomas. I can't believe I finally found you."

My heart swelled, my eyes filled with tears and before I knew it my hands where in his hair and my lips were crushing into his, his hands wrapped around my waist and pulled me into him. The kiss was deep and hungry and hot!

My hands ran through his hair pulling him closer to me and deeper into the kiss while he gripped my shirt and waist and held me against him so there wasn't an inch between us. I think I would have been lost to him forever if I wasn't brought back to reality with the sound of cheering and wolf whistles. He was the first to pull away and I realised the noise was for us. I could feel everyone's eyes on us as they cheered, whooped and whistled.

"For Maker's sake." I covered my eyes in embarrassment. "I'm so sorry," but as I looked up at him again he was smiling, grinning from ear to ear and looking down at me and out to the crowd.

I don't think I'd ever seen anything so magnificent.

His happiness was infectious and I couldn't help but start giggling like a teenager. I slowly turned around to see everyone at the party staring at us and in turn they started their cheering up again.

You'd think I was the town spinster or something. Oh wait, I am.

My father eventually told everyone to go about their business and let us get on with it, but this just seemed to add a more considerable amount of pressure to the situation.

I was now facing away from him again, and the thought of turning back to face him was filling me with anxiety. He leaned next to me against the railings and looked out over the yard, we were so close but it was still too far away. I wanted nothing more than to have our bodies intertwined again and have his arms wrapped around me, but once again I was glued to the spot, he had glued me to the spot.

"Any particular reason you don't want me to move?" I said, still not looking at him.

He leant in so only I could hear. "Miss Thomas, I feel if you were to move then something very inappropriate would happen right here on your parent's porch in front all these people. So to save your dignity I'm going to have to insist you stay where you are for the time being."

I could feel the energy rolling off of him in waves, he wanted everything I did and possibly more, but he was right, this was neither the time nor the place. So instead, we just looked out over the party. I pointed out my family members and told him bits about the people I knew. Every now and then someone came over to congratulate me, forcing me to explain the fact that on the commune I was considered an eternal spinster to still be without a family at my age, which made him oddly sad. It filled him with something I couldn't quit pin down, it's possible he just felt bad for me but it seemed more, much more.

Chapter Seventeen

Now the party was in full swing and it was reaching 3am. The moonshine was flowing, the fire pit was ablaze and everyone was feeling the effects of Samhain.

You see, to us, Samhain is a bit like a mating season, it's not that we don't mate at any other time it's just that everything is so heightened that it just makes everyone that little bit extra erotically charged than they are the rest of the year. So, by default most of our young are conceived around Samhain. Now in previous years I'd never really felt the full effects of Samhain but tonight, tonight I was feeling them. Standing next to this Adonis all evening and feeling the passion and lust roll off of him in waves, not to mention my inexplicable desire to climb him like a tree and rip his clothes off, made for a very super charged evening indeed. Every time we touched by accident or unexpectedly looked into each other's eyes the air filled will so much tension it made others instantly uncomfortable and they usually made their excuses to move on as quickly as they could.

I wanted to be alone with him but at the same time dreaded the thought of it, what would we do if we were alone?

I know exactly what we'd do!

But that was the problem, I didn't know if I was ready to go there with him. I barely knew him and apart from the odd occasion we'd mainly been rude or very awkward towards each other, and even though our connection was undeniable I still felt I needed to know him more, to understand him.

As I stood there staring at this beautiful Adonis playing ball with some of the commune kids, who had pestered him as he was for sure the biggest person there, to get their ball out of a tree and then insisted he played with them. All I could think is that I wanted to know everything, I wanted to know all there was to know about Eli Alutiiq and I wanted him to know me, truly know me, the kind of knowing that took forever and that's when it hit me… He's mine… He's my mate.

Now that thought, as much as it filled me with unbelievable joy, also started a very unforgiving panic attack. All I could think was that I need some fresh air and space but as I was already outside in the yard; I did the opposite and sneakily made my way into the house.

I hoped that no one would see me as some breathing space was definitely what was needed at this point. I headed for the kitchen but found some stragglers had set up camp in there so followed my feet to my room instead.

Over the years it had become a sanctuary to me, yeah it was way too small, and yeah, I really needed to move out, but it wasn't something Mystics really did until they had a mate to move in with.

Oh Maker, stop thinking about it!

I pulled on one of my less flattering sweaters as it was massive and warm and the temperature had started to dip, and then sat on my bed. I'm not really sure how long I sat there, but I just sat. I mainly tried not to let myself think about anything. After a while I remembered my box, the one my father had given me earlier that evening. I knelt beside my bed and pulled it out from where I'd hidden it before and once again it began to hum for me, I almost felt like I recognised the tune but it was so faint it couldn't quit grasp it. I let my fingers float around the engravings once more and decided now was the time.

I ran my hands around the lid and realised I didn't know how to open it. It didn't have a lid like a normal box, or hinges, or a lock, no it was just a large cube. By the weight of it, it definitely wasn't a solid block but how it opened I had no idea. I tried a few silly things to open it, knocking, open sesame, asking politely, that kind of thing; but none of them worked… Obviously. So I then tried to open it with magic. I tried to open it as I was opening a door and then a lock but nothing, I tried a few more things, whatever I could think of really and nothing. I sat

studying it for some time to see if I could understand
anything on it but no luck, it was completely alien to me.
Then I heard his voice, he called to me from downstairs
and my heart sprang to life followed by the box springing
open. It opened out like a flower, suddenly the hard wood
had become more like soft brown petals that floated back
to reveal its contents. Inside was a ring, an ornate antique
brass filigree band with an opal stone set into it. On first
glance it could have been a child's dress-up ring but on
closer inspection it was far from it. Encrusted into the band
was what looked like hundreds of tiny diamonds and the
opal looked like it had the galaxy floating within it. When I
picked it up it weighed heavy in my hands, but with magic
not actual weight. The ring itself was light as a feather but
I could feel the magic resonating from it, and oddly I
recognised it. It felt familiar to me, like I'd known magic
like this before. I slipped the ring on the ring finger of my
right hand and held it out in front of my face, it was a
genuinely beautiful ring, a bit bigger and flashier than I
would have picked, but beautiful none the less. Something
within the stone suddenly seemed to start moving and as I
looked closer a small burst of light came from the centre of
it and it changed colour, it was now a bright red and was
what looked like smoke swirling around inside of it. Then
I felt him.

"There you are, I've been looking for you everywhere."

I stared at him for a moment and then back at the ring, I knew somehow it changed because of him.

"Evelyn? Are you okay?" he asked kneeling down next to me.

"Yes. Sorry. I just needed some space. I mean fresh air. I mean… I just needed a minute. Sorry." I blushed.

What an idiot.

"Oh, I'll leave you to it then. Sorry, I was just worried about you."

"No, please, stay?"

Eloquent as always, Evelyn.

He looked so cute and pleased that I'd asked him to stay. Him lighting up like a little boy made my heart soar and it was all I could do not to throw myself at him. I think he picked up on my thoughts as he shifted where he knelt and appeared to blush a little.

Aww, your turn, Big Boy!

I smiled as sweetly as I could to let him know I wasn't going to act on it, but I did reach out and hold his hand. It seemed like a silly gesture but I needed to touch him, I wanted much more in fact, but for now, this would do. I was looking down at our hands when I realised my ring had changed colour.

"Hey, it changes colour. How does it do that?" he asked picking my hand up and bringing it to his face for a better look. This time it had turned the deepest amber, like a beautiful gemstone, it turned into his eye colour. The sight of it filled me with such incredible happiness, I could feel my eyes welling up at the thought of it, I felt like it knew the two of us, like it was a part of me, like it had been missing from my hand all these years, like he was missing from my heart.

"Is that… is that my eye colour?" he asked while giving it and me the most confused look.

I nodded "I think so, yeah."

"How is that possible? Have you spelled it to do that or something?"

"No, I don't really know how it works. It was left to me in this box of things. My father gave them to me last night."

"Last night? Why'd he wait so long?"

"Apparently he had strict instructions to wait until the time was right."

"And last night was the right time?"

"I guess so."

"Why?"

"You."

"Me?"

This could go on for a while…

"Yes, you." I giggled. He looked completely shocked. "What do I have to do with all this?"

I suddenly become beyond embarrassed and my panic attack started to rear up again. How could I talk to him of being my mate and forever when we'd never even been on a date, we didn't even know each other for Maker's sake. I was now crimson from head to toe and I couldn't think of a single thing to say.

"Evelyn? Are you okay?"

All I could do was nod.

Smooth!

The ring was now a bright shade of solid pink.

I think I'm getting the idea now.

"Evelyn, please. I don't want you to feel embarrassed in front of me," he said running his hand along my cheek and holding my face. It was an incredible feeling.

He pulled my gaze up to meet his and he just looked into my eyes and took a deep breath. "I don't know if I'll ever get used to looking at you," he said with a smile beaming down at me. "I know this all seems insane and I know we don't know each other but I feel like I've known you forever and… I'm sorry. Evelyn, I am truly sorry for the way I have behaved recently and although there should be no excuse for my actions towards you and your family I hope you can understand that they were not my true intent and I pray you can see I was just in a bad place, we were just in a bad place." He had the most pained look on his face, it broke my heart to see him hurting. I reached up and put my hands on either side of his face, rose to my knees and pulled his gaze to meet mine. He was hurting and all I wanted to do was make it better.

"How can I help? Tell me what I can do to help?"

"Help? After the way I've treated you, you want to help me?" he gave a half laugh. He pulled me into his chest and kissed the top of my head "I can't believe I found you."

I soaked in the moment, afraid to move in case it came to an end. His body engulfed mine, he was huge compared to me, and he resembled a bear even in human form.

Oh yeah, he's a bear. How does that work?

"As much as I don't want to let you go, I should probably be getting back at some point, I've been gone nearly 24 hours."

I wanted to tell him no, I wanted to tell him to stay with me and never let me go but instead I just sat back and smiled. "I understand," is all I could muster. I didn't.

He placed a soft kiss on my head and rose to his feet. "Can I see you later today? I can come back here, or will you be back to The Lodge? Or anywhere, I can meet you anywhere you wish."

"Yes," I said smiling, "of course you can, I should probably get back to work today anyhow."

"No one would blame you for taking a few days."

"At Samhain? No, no, no, too much to do. I have the Alutiiq booking to take care of remember?" I said with a wink.

"Ah, I see. Yes, well, best crack to it then, I hear they can be a bit of a handful."

I laughed "Yes especially one of the brothers, he's a complete pain in my ass."

He laughed, gave me a quick wink and another kiss on the head and left. I stared after him for some time after he'd gone, then I remembered my box. I looked back down at the ring, it was now a wispy light blue, which was oddly exactly how I felt. "So you're a mood ring, huh? How very 1990s of you." it swirled as I spoke to it, something told me it was no ordinary mood ring.

Along with the ring were some documents, one was my birth certificate. It was of course a Mystic version and it was the first time I'd ever seen it, the first time I'd even thought about it if I'm honest. And there he was, penned out in front of me in perfect calligraphy: Sebastian Thomas, my father apparently. I had never had any information about them and I'd never really wanted it. It just seemed easier that way. Can't miss what you never had and all that. But where my mother's name should have been there were just initials- BD. How strange. Why would they only put the initials? I ran my fingers over the letters, tracing them as I went. "BD," as I said them out loud my ring turned a glorious emerald green, it swished and swirled with the deepest, most beautiful greens and settled to rest on a deep emerald with wisps of amber running through it, it almost looked like eyes. It filled me with a sense of sentiment that maybe my mother and I shared the same eye colour and it was of course possible, but it was only the musings of an old ring, it could have been showing me anything. I also discovered I was born in Maine, interesting I guess, finding out facts about myself I never knew. It also had the basics, my weight, time of birth etc. etc. but it also had some writing on the back. I flipped it over to see what it said but it was in a dialect I didn't understand, it seemed similar to what was on the box itself but this was hand written. I studied it for a few moments to see if I could recognise any of the symbols but no such luck, so I moved on.

Next on the pile was a piece of scrap paper, it looked like it might have been from a page in a book. As I stared at it I could feel it pulling at me, lulling me in. It wanted me to pick it up, but I hesitated, it wasn't an overly reassuring sign when a piece of paper had an agenda. I hovered my hand over it to see if my ring reacted and to it and it did, it turned a piercing bright blue with bursts of white and looked as if it almost glowed. The colour didn't seem threatening at all, it was very appealing actually, almost angelic. I reached out to pick up the piece of paper but it fluttered away from me, so again I tried grab it but it again fluttered away. I pretended to give up for a moment and then quickly grabbed it in my right hand "ha-ha!" I shouted when suddenly my hand felt like an elephant had sat in it. The scrap piece of paper felt as though it weighed a tonne and sent my hand crashing into the floor, on impact a pile of dust blew up in my face as though it was a dusty old tome in the back of a library, and to my utter surprise, it was. When I looked down again it was now a very large, very dusty hard backed book, well, tome, it would definitely be described as a tome. I eyed the book suspiciously. I didn't seem to be menacing but you never can be too sure with old boys like this, they seem normal and book-like then suddenly you've opened a gateway to hell, or something equally as ominous.

I ran my fingers over the face of the book and the same thing happened as when I had touched the box, it hummed to me, a silent vibration in the air but I could definitely hear it, it was humming, a beautiful, slightly ethereal tune. It soothed me deep inside, a warming feeling crept through me as if I was laying in the sun, it was exquisite. I opened the book at a random page and there was a picture of a woman dressed in full length silver robes, they seemed to be made of one individual strand of string, one long glittering strand scantily covered her body and she was holding the end piece in her left hand and held an hourglass in the other. She was vaguely familiar to me but I couldn't place her. She was beautiful though, one of the most beautiful women I'd ever seen. She had long, jet black hair flowing down to her waist and piercing blue eyes that looked almost white. She shared the picture with two other women, but they were in the distance with their backs turned, and a snake curled around itself with the end of it draped over her right foot. It was a stunning picture, the kind that you'd imagine as part of a supernatural collection, there was a page full of writing adjacent to it but it was in the same dialect as before so I had no hope of understanding it. I turned a few pages and saw more pictures of more beautiful men and women, all with different themes for their portraits. I assumed it was some sort of art history book for Mystics but I had no idea, and nor would I until I figured out what language everything was written in.

There was one further piece of paper and an envelope within the box, the piece of paper was written in the same language and the envelope was addressed to me. I opened the envelope and hoped it wasn't also written in the same script. It wasn't, and at first glance I didn't know whether to laugh or cry.

To my darling Evelyn,

> *I hope this letter finds you happy and well. I'm sure you have so many question about all this and I'm sorry I can't be there to answer them for you but unfortunately our time together has had to come to an end. I so wished I could have watched you grow and become whoever you are, I bet the Maker you'd be a hell of a woman, and if your father has anything to do with it you'll be a force to be reckoned with.*

I'm so sorry that all of this had to fall on you, but I promise it will be over one day and you can have the normal life your father always wanted for you. If I had anything to do with it, however, you'd be the Grand Supreme by the time you were 200! But that's a long way off and you have a long way to go, and much to learn about yourself before you need to worry about any of that. You must be so excited now that your training can start, I wish I could see what you are capable of. I hope you and your mate are happy, and I hope he's a beast! Not an actual Beast, but I guess that would be okay, just so long as he's good for you I'll be happy.

I hope you're dad hasn't been too much of a slave driver, he can be a bore at times. All rules and regulations, and no fun (well not all rules, you're proof of that, oops, don't tell him I said that!) Just make sure you keep him in check, he needs to have fun once in a while. Make him take you to the fountains, if he hasn't already, he loves the fountains, it was where we met. But I digress, I guess this letter has to end somewhere and it might as well be here...

I'm so sorry, my darling girl, I never wanted this for you, for any of us, but this is what must be. I hope you understand that everything we have done is to protect you and because we love you with everything we have. Listen to your father and look

*out for him too, he has a knack for finding
trouble... hence me.*

*I love you, Evie, with all that I am, with all that
I have, and with all that I will be, I love you.*

*May the Maker watch over you and your father
and bless your new union with love and life from
this day forward.*

Forever your loving mother, Ban

I sat for a moment trying to take in what I'd just read but it
didn't seem to sink in. Maybe because it didn't make any
sense to me. I thought my parents had died together in an
accident but this makes it sound like I was left with my
father. Was my mother ill? Did she just leave? Was she
taken away? Why was I left with my father and where is
he now? Did he actually die or has he left me as well? For
all I couldn't make out in this letter, there was one thing
that rang out to me... my mother may still be alive.

Chapter Eighteen

I lay in bed trying not to let my brain dwell on all that flooded it. It had been a rather eventful day after all, and it had followed a rather intense week. If I'm honest I needed some proper rest but it seemed an impossible task lately. My head was endlessly bombarded with thoughts of my parents, who I was, where they were, what happened to them, succubae attacks, will he come back for me again, why he won't leave me alone, and the biggest thought of all, the one consuming most of my consciousness… Eli Alutiiq. He filled my head at every opportune moment, every time I stopped thinking for a moment he slipped in, never really leaving my mind at all. I wonder what took us so long to find each other, my mother obviously assumed that we would meet young, like most. But it had taken us over two centuries, seems odd. I wonder what he's doing now, I tried to picture him, to imagine what he was up to. I mindlessly stared at my ring whilst I thought of him, and as I did it slowly turned into his colour, the deep amber soared around inside the ring until it looked like the perfect replica of his eyes, then I could see him. Not in front of me like he was there in the room but I could see him in my mind. I knew what he was doing. He was in bear form and running, pounding through woodlands, charging strong and powerful like the "beast" he is. Such odd words for my mother to use in her letter, *"I hope he's a beast"*. I wonder what made her use it. Not that I'm complaining, he is a beast and I love it.

Oops, careful with the L word, Thomas.

I watched him in my mind's eye pounding through the forest, he was large and heavy but fast and agile at the same time. He moved with swift direct movements as he charged forward. I wondered if I could actually see him or if it was just my imagination, so I concentrated harder, I wanted to see if it was real. And suddenly there it was. My whole body hummed with electricity as if he was in bed next to me.

That's a dangerous thought.

My whole body trembled with desire for him as though he was in the room, I could feel him, I could really feel him. In his bear form he was different, still him but altered slightly. His animal was a part of him always, and I could always feel its presence when I was around him. It was his primal side, it was powerful and domineering and admittedly a little frightening, but this felt different. He was angry, and not in a normal way. I could feel waves of blinding rage coming off of him, it consumed him, ate away at his whole being and now mine. I could feel what he felt. Blinding white rage stung my eyes as I began to sob. My body buckled with the pain and heartache he was feeling. Not being able to take anymore I pulled myself back, pulled my mind and emotions away from him. It was one of the hardest things I have ever had to do, it took everything I had to push him out. Just before we disconnected he let out a pain filled thunderous roar. I recoiled from him into my bed covers and sobbed for some time.

I must have cried myself to sleep as the next thing I knew it was morning and my phone was buzzing somewhere in the pile of things from the night before. I scrambled around for my phone and heard that the party was sizzling out but still going downstairs. Finally finding my phone I had nine missed calls from Pierre. I sagged on the spot. I know I said I was going in today but Maker I didn't want to. As I sat looking around the mess in my room I let myself muse about the possibilities from the night before, about my history, about Eli, about my mother. Before I could indulge for too long my phone started to buzz in my hand, it was Pierre again.

"Hello," I said with as much enthusiasm I could muster.

"'Allo, my darling. 'Ow are you feeling?"

"Yeah, I'm good," is all I could manage right now. I wanted to say nothing, because that's kind of how I felt, nothing. It was the strangest feeling; or lack of.

"Good to 'ear my, darling. Um… as much as I don' want to bozer you, we 'ave a bit of a situation 'ere."

"What do you mean? What kind of situation?"

"I'm sorry, my darling, I zink you need to come see for yourself."

My whole body sank. All I could think was the worst. What could have possibly happened, they only had casual plans last night, everyone was prepared, and nothing could have gone wrong.

"I'll be right there," is all I could get out before hanging up the phone. It took everything I had to get up and get myself ready. Showering and dressing had never been such a chore. When I was finally ready I headed downstairs. As I reached the front room loud cheering and wolf whistling erupted. I jumped out of my skin, well I would have if could feel anything, I don't know what it was but I was completely numb. For something that would normally make me jump for the rafters and scream like a girl, barely gave me a startle. I was numb.

"Heeey, there she is. Is he still up there then?" Jimmy shouted walking over and putting his arm over my shoulder. Everyone laughed and cheered.

"I'm sorry what?" in my confused numbness I just wasn't getting the joke.

"Your date from last night," he said winking at me with a massive grin. "The one and only Mr Eli Alutiiq. Is he still up there or has he slipped out the front door?" A few more deep "wheys" and loud laughter followed.

"I'm sorry I don't know what you're talking abo… oh," I would usually have gone a deep shade of crimson at this point but nothing, not even a flush.

Who am I?

"I'm sorry to disappoint you, folks, but just me up there." Everyone booed and I decided I didn't need any breakfast, even though I did. I headed for the car anyway. Jimmy followed me out "Hey, Evie, wait up."

I stopped just in front of my car.

"Is everything okay? I thought you guys… You know… *Really* hit it off?" he over-emphasized the really.

"Well, yeah we did. I think." My mind was so foggy and confused.

"Okay, well… Are you okay?"

"Yeah I think so," I said in the flattest tone I'd ever heard.

"You don't seem okay," he said examining me.

"Yeah, I know, sorry, I'm just totally out of it. I think I just need some sleep."

"Then stay home, they can do without you for one day, Evie, after everything that's happened, you need to rest."

"Well apparently they can't. Pierre called there's been some incident or situation, or something… I don't know. He just needs me down there." I opened my car door and practically fell in.

"If there's a problem then let me come with you, maybe I can help."

"No its fine, it won't be anything big. I'll call if I need you, okay?" I closed the car door and drove off leaving Jimmy in the driveway starring after me with worry etched into his face.

Chapter Nineteen

When I arrived at The Lodge it was clear something serious was wrong. The whole place was a ghost town. It wasn't normally busy at the front entrance but the whole place had lost its buzz, it felt flat and empty when it was normally buzzing with the feel of life. My heart sank.

Maker, what's happened?

I rounded the corner to the staff parking and found Pierre waiting for me at my space. He looked drawn and agonised. I stepped out of the car and he came round to great me. He scooped me up in a friendly embrace. "My darling, 'ow are you?"

"Yeah, fine, Pierre. What's going on?"

He set me down and gave me the most troubled look. He said no more and just grabbed my hand and led me off. He first took me around the building to the tennis courts, I couldn't believe my eyes. It looked like a bomb had gone off inside it. Windows were smashed, doors were hanging of their hinges, and the inside was totally destroyed. "What happened here?" I said in astonishment as I looked over the building.

"Wait, zere's more," he said leading me off again, this time to the side of the main building where the terrace came out to the gardens from the ballroom. My hand shot to my mouth and my eyes stung with tears. It was almost demolished. Every single pane of glass was smashed, every single one of the two hundred and thirty stained glass panes that made up the terrace garden was now nothing but sand.

"What happened here, Pierre? What the hell happened?" for the life of me I couldn't think of one single scenario that could possibly explain this. My life's work, my home, my family.

"Oh, Maker, is everyone okay? Is anybody hurt?"

Oh, Maker, let them all be okay.

"I don' really know all the details," he said looking dubious. "They made me promise to bring you straight to zem when you got 'ere." He started to lead me off again. I was going to ask who, but that would be a stupid question. I knew exactly who we were going to see, but at least I knew he had nothing to do with it, I knew where he had been last night. A slight flutter came over me at the thought of him but it was quickly suppressed by my numbness, something was telling me to prepare myself for what was coming next.

Pierre walked me up to the pool bar, I could already see that it had been commandeered by the Alutiiq Clan. Even through the tinted glass you could see all the giant bodies filling the room. I braced myself and let Pierre open the door for me. As soon as it opens I pulled myself up, slapped a half smile on my face and strode across the room. It was almost earie in here, they all seemed so sombre. Some looked at me with pitying looks, some with something else. I couldn't quit pin down the mood in here, which was odd, I could normally feel out a room the second I got near it.

I marched myself up to the centre of the room where the heads of the family had congregated with Lady Alutiiq right in the centre of everything, she was chatting in hushed voices to an older gentleman next to her, as I walked over she fell silent and looked up at me with a very torn expression. "Good afternoon, Miss Thomas, won't you please sit." It wasn't a question, it was an instruction, but I appreciated the pretence of it.

"Tell me, dear, how are you feeling?" she asked while bringing a cup of tea to her lips, taking the daintiest of sips and then returning it back to its saucer.

"I'm fine, thank you for asking," I said slapping on my work smile for her.

"Well this is surprising, after the week you've had, no?" she said taking another sip of tea. I felt like it was supposed to be some sort of intimidation technique but I didn't really get it.

"I suppose it might be, but I assure you I am fine."

"Well how wonderful," she said with the driest tone. "I can't imagine what has you feeling so *"fine"*, as you put it," she said shooting daggers from over her tea cup to the corner of the room. I didn't think before I looked. Her act had caught my interest and I followed her gaze to where she had looked, and there he stood, like a heavenly giant in the far corner of the room, my heart skipped a beat and I fidgeted in my chair as I looked back at Lady Alutiiq.

Big Mistake!

She caught something in my eye and I think I gave her the confirmation she had been looking for.

Crap on a cracker!

I don't know why but I knew this was bad. The fact that Eli refused to make eye contact with me when I looked at him, the rage that he was in earlier and, the fact that he is stood as far away from us as possible… yeah, I think there's definitely a problem.

I looked her square on, I didn't let my gaze falter, I knew if I showed her even the slightest weakness she would tear me apart.

"Well, now we've established I'm fine, can we discuss the… The condition of The Lodge, shall we say?" I said still not letting my gaze falter.

"Yes, well that. That is where I pass the podium to Charlton, he has insisted that I let him tell you, well so be it, but it will be here in front of the Court that it is discussed, not in private as you requested." She addressed the end to Charlton.

"But, My Lady, please, to save the girl some dignity, please let us talk in private?"

"I don't see how she has any dignity left to be saved," she said shooting me a look of disgust.

"Excuse me? What in Maker's name…? What on earth could this be, that it requires a Court, and why does the Court require my dignity to be on trial?" I was beyond angry. How dare she? Who does she think she is? I started to tremble with rage. Needless to say my gaze had now faltered and turned into something resembling a deranged harpy. I don't think I'd ever felt this way before, no one had ever managed to bring this out of me the way she was right now. And the numbness I'd felt earlier had been replaced with anger.

"Miss Thomas, please, forgive our approach, you must understand that this is just protocol," Charlton said gesturing to the room. "We do not mean to cause you any more distress than you have already had to suffer, but this is apparently the only way."

"The only way what, Charlton? What is going on!?" I was filling with more and more rage as they prolonged the inevitable.

Charlton moved to sit next to me and took my hands. "Miss Thomas, in the early hours of this morning a clan of succubae turned up here looking for you. They started by surrounding the Lodge and demanded we hand you over. When no one responded they… They stormed The Lodge. If we hadn't been out at the house I don't know what would have happened, but luckily, we were. We managed to overpower them from the outside. It got pretty close though, they came at us pretty heavy. If Eli hadn't shown up when he did, I don't know what would have happened." He said shooting his lap a pained look.

"Is everybody okay? Did anyone get hurt?" I said with tears stinging my eyes. Charlton gave me a soft smile. "Yes, Miss Thomas, everyone is fine, apart from a few nicks and scratches and some very questionable stories, everyone is fine." He always had a way of making me smile, he was so gentle. He stared at me as if waiting for me to say something. "Miss Thomas," he said eyeing me delicately. "They came here for you. Do you maybe have some questions about that?"

"Oh, I just assumed it was related to the other night… No?" I said looking around me as everyone seemed to still.

"Well, yes I guess it is," he said giving me those pained eyes again. "Miss Thomas, they came for you because they think that you now belong to them…" He seemed to need a moment before he said what was next… "Miss Thomas. Evelyn, they believe you are… In incubation." I froze. My entire body went cold, stone cold, and now more than ever I wanted that numbness to slip back over me but it didn't, it just left me hanging out to face it on my own. My heart was pounding in my chest, I could hear it loud and clear, and I could feel bile rising in my throat.

Don't you dare, not now. If I'm sick in front these people I will never recover.

I kept repeating *"no weakness"* in my head to try and keep myself from vomiting. It wasn't easy. My brain ran riots trying to remember what had happened that night. How could this be? There's no way I can be in incubation. Pregnant? No way, it can't be. I would know… Wouldn't I? Charlton took my hand once more.

"Am I?" Is all I could manage.

"No! Oh no, Evelyn. Sorry, I maybe should have lead with that. I would be able to tell if you were. And as far as we can tell, you are most definitely not. But that doesn't stop them from thinking so. They think the only reason we would have killed their disgusting little friend is if he had succeeded in his task. However we felt his fate was sewn the moment he came back here."

I sat trying to process what he'd said.

"Miss Thomas, are you okay?"

I looked him in the eyes and saw how pained they were and I couldn't help it, I laughed. I laughed loud!

"Okay?" I managed to squeeze out in between snorts. "Are you serious, Charlton? What part of this whole scenario do you think I might be okay with?" I was losing the funny side now.

He just nodded. "I'm so sorry. You're right. That was an inconsiderate question, Miss Thomas, I do not, on any level, wish to diminish what has happened to you. I sincerely apologise." He looked up at me with the most apologetic face I'd ever seen.

"Charlton, it is not your place to be apologising to this girl, you are not the reason she is in this mess," said Lady Alutiiq looking disgustedly down her nose at me.

"Thank you for your input, Lady Alutiiq, but I think we have safely established what you think of me, so no further proof of that will be necessary," I said as calmly as I could, but this was starting to break me now, I could feel myself becoming more and more out of control. "Now, hopefully, you can all understand that this is somewhat devastating news, so please enlighten me on why it needed to be done with a Court witness?" I said, trying to keep my voice from wavering. Lady Alutiiq was spitting daggers at me but there was also a gleam in her eye, I couldn't put my finger on what is was there for, but it was definitely there.

The older gentleman sat next to Lady Alutiiq finally stood. "Miss Thomas, you appear in front of our Courts today charged with gross misconduct in the use of magic. How do you plead?"

"How do I plead? Wait, what?" I racked my brains but I couldn't make any sense of all this.

What the Maker are they talking about?

"I'm sorry but you're going to have to explain what you're referring to. I'm afraid I have absolutely no idea what's going on anymore."

"Miss Thomas you are charged with practising forbidden forms of magic and creating an Amour-Mendacium upon a member of this Court."

"An Amour-Mendacium? A love spell? Who on earth would I…" Then I realised what was happening. My eyes glued to my hands in my lap while tears threatened my eyes and bile rose in my throat.

"You were saying?" pipped up Lady Alutiiq with what could only be described as glee in her voice.

Bitch!

I look up at her and we lock eyes. Neither of us wavered. I wanted to launch myself at her, I wanted to suck up all the energy in the room and blast it in her stupid smug face, but I knew I couldn't. In a Court like this I would most likely be executed for such a crime, these clans take their Courts and their matriarchs very seriously.

After some time of staring her down she finally looked away and I think I even managed to make her uncomfortable.

Good!

I looked up at the man who had been addressing the Court and it took everything I had to keep my voice from wavering. "I would like to hear the testimony from the victim," I said sounding strong and confident.

Don't know how I'm pulling this off.

"What?" He spat almost falling over himself. Murmurs and gasps filled the room.

"Um… Well yes, of course." He looked genuinely shocked at my request. They knew they were full of it and they expected me to just roll over and take it, well apparently not today, today I was a glutton for punishment and I wanted to hear what madness they had concocted.

"The Court calls Eli Alutiiq to witness," he bellowed out to the room.

"That won't be necessary," Lady Alutiiq quickly threw in. "My Grandson is very distraught over the matter and does not wish to discuss it any further. However…," she added with way too much pleasure, whilst pulling out a letter from her purse. "I have a signed statement from Eli explaining everything, if you care to read it?" she said throwing me a smile on the end.

Don't push me, lady.

"I think given the circumstances I have every right to hear what the *victim* has to say. I deserve to know the exact reason I am being charged, do I not?" I knew my rights here and I knew they couldn't refuse me if they wanted to keep things kosher.

"Very well. Eli Alutiiq, the Court calls you!" bellowed the speaker from before.

He didn't move. He seemed like he wasn't even in the room, he was completely vacant. The jerk's making me look like a complete fool and he can't even be bothered to pay attention.

Charming as ever then.

What is his game? If he thinks I'm going to just let him get out of this scot free he's got another thing coming. We were over before we'd even begun, that was painfully clear to see now, but if he thinks I'm going to just roll over any play dead, he is most certainly mistaken.

"Eli Alutiiq!?" the speaker bellowed again, this time in his direction.

He seemed to come back to the room with a thud. "What?" was apparently all he could manage.

"The Court calls you," the speaker said with much more disdain than seemed necessary.

"What for?" he said seeming confused about the situation. He shot his grandmother a quick glare and she responded with a shrug.

He reluctantly approached the area we were sat and took the piece of paper.

"What's this?" he said eyeing it.

Lady Alutiiq gave a nervous glance around the room. "It's your statement, *remember*?" she said emphasising the "remember".

That was when he finally looked up.

Shit.

He looked beyond broken. His face was etched deep with pain, his eyes dull and lifeless and he looked at me as though it might kill him to do so. My heart finally broke. I was so busy being angry about the situation I never actually accepted its true meaning. They're doing all this to me, a stranger they want gone, but they're also doing it to him. They're his family, could it really be so bad that we are meant for union?

I could feel my bravado fading, falling apart around me. I was doing okay when I was just angry, that was easy, but now… Now I'm breaking.

Seeing him like that nearly destroyed me, was slowly destroying me. And then suddenly none of this made any sense. If he didn't want this to happen, why are they doing this? Why would I need to be removed?

Lady Alutiiq cleared her throat, it was only then I realised how long we'd been staring at each other. People were paying more attention now, it had suddenly become interesting, like a good T.V. drama.

He finally turned his head to look at her.

"Read your statement, dear," she said with an edge to her voice. "Read it!" she followed with when he didn't immediately start.

He unfolded the document and glanced over the wording. It was so very subtle but every few seconds you could see his face grimace.

"What's the matter, boy?" said the speaker looking impatient. "Is this not your statement?"

Please say no! Please say no! Please say no!

Lady Alutiiq locked eyes with him and started to reach for her purse. He quickly looked up to the speaker and declared it was his. "Yeah-yes, it's mine." He had resigned himself to our fate.

Maker take me.

"Well then read it!" he demanded.

I could feel all that was left of my bravado slipping away. I was done. I had to get out of here and fast.

He looked down and took a deep controlled breath and prepared to read.

"Wait!" I yelled in a bit of a blind panic. As much as I wanted to see what he had to say for himself I couldn't bear to hear it. "I don't need to hear it," I blurted. Knowing he was willing to read it told me enough. "If that is all? I'd very much like to leave now." I stood and turned to leave but was met by two large men who blocked my path. One of them was the big guy I had frozen on the day they arrived. He gave a half smile and half sorry look. "I'm going to assume that is not all." I turned around and slowly sat back in my chair.

"Miss Thomas, Court is still in session. Now, do you understand the terms under which you are charged?" said the speaker to room in general.

"Okay, so… I am being charged with spelling this man…" I go to look at him but I can't, he won't let me.

How dare he control me now?

"…With an Amour-Mendacium, a love spell, and interfering with the bond of the sacred union? Is that correct?" I ask.

"Yes, Miss Thomas. That is correct," he says without looking at me. "How do you plead?"

I take a moment to think about it. Moments ago I was ready to admit the lie and go along with all the madness just so I could get out of here, but I just couldn't, I couldn't allow these bullies to do this to me without a fight. He and I are clearly done, but I will not be treated this way, especially not in my own home. "Let the Court hear me when I say this," I stand up and raise my voice just enough so that the room can hear me. "I have not and would not disgrace our sacred union in such a way. I, as all of you, hold it with great regard and respect. I honestly believed that what happened between Mr Alutiiq and myself was that of a devoted union, but given this display here today I see that it was not. I apologise for my naivety and can vow to you now that it will not be a problem for you any longer. Mr Alutiiq clearly has no interest in me and obviously feels pained about the situation, and I shall certainly not be pursuing the matter any further, so… In answer to your questions… I plead not guilty." I stand tall and use everything I have to stop myself from collapsing into a blithering heap on the floor.

"Miss Thomas, the court has heard your statement and will now adjourn to deliberate the proceedings. You are free to leave but we request that you stay in the vicinity so we can easily reach you."

"Sure," is all I can muster.

Chapter Twenty

I fly out of there as fast as my heels can carry me, but it isn't fast enough. As soon as my face hits the fresh air I disappear. I appear a moment later in my spot in the woods. Although it has been forever tarnished for me now, it was the only place I could think to go where I could be alone.

My knees crumple and I hit the ground with a thud. My body heaves with breath taking sobs. I curl into a ball at the edge of the stream and sob till my sides hurt. I can feel that my face is swollen and my voice has become harsh. I have no idea how long I've been out here but I figure people would understand my absence. As the tears started to slow I gradually bought myself up to a sitting position. I flung my feet in front of me, took off my shoes, and let my feet dip into the stream. I could feel it healing me. Restoring everything I'd lost over the last few hours, few days maybe.

I hear a rustle behind me and I know my time alone is over. I feel Charlton enter the clearing, his emotions flooding off of him as he approaches. He just stands and waits. I presume he's waiting for me to make the first move.

Might be a while.

"Charlton, if you're going to insist on being here then please get a grip on your emotions, my own are enough to contend with at the moment, thank you."

"My apologies, Miss Thomas. I didn't want to disturb you."

"Pleeeease stop apologising to me, Charlton, and for the last time, call me Evelyn!" I demanded. I still haven't looked at him. I'm afraid I might resort back to uncontrollable sobbing if I see the look on his face. He sits down next to me at the edge of the brook. His form engulfs me. I never really realised how big he was. He was always so calm and collected, and smaller than… Some of the others, that I never really saw it before. I shivered in his shadow and he quickly took off his jacket and wrapped it around my shoulders.

"I am so sorry, Evelyn." I went to protest the apology but he raised his hand to silence me, "Please… let me finish," he said closing his eyes. "Evelyn, over my many years I have seen my clan, my family, do some very unsavoury things, and some very… Appalling things. I have questioned them, I have argued with them, and I have ignored them. But up until today I have never actually hated them. I always found some sort of explanation, no matter how feeble, to their actions. But today, today I cannot find one. What they did to you I cannot explain nor understand. So from the bottom of my heart, and of the hearts of those of us that feel the same way, I am so very sorry, more sorry than I could ever explain. And now… Now I make to you a promise, a promise to help you in any way I can and to do all I can to fix what my family has broken." I knew he was talking about Eli and me, but all I could think was that there wasn't anything to fix. I sagged next to him, my body struggling to hold itself up. I was completely exhausted and struggling to fight it.

"Come, let's get you some rest shall we, we have much to discuss but all can wait till you're rested." He slipped an arm around me and hoisted me to my feet. I appeared to be walking but really he was just carrying me, and I let him. It wasn't until I saw where we were heading that I put up a fight, a meagre one, but still. "No, Charlton. I will not go in there. There is plenty of room for me elsewhere," I say whilst trying to struggle pointlessly against his arms.

"Mis-Evelyn, there is nowhere else. Most of the staff accommodation was trashed during the Succubae attack and your staff are in all your vacant rooms. Please, Evelyn, we can look after you here. We have prepared a room for you. Please, let us help you." I wanted to fight him on it, I wanted to storm off and refuse any such help, but I couldn't, I didn't have it in me to stand up, let alone argue or fight with him, so I just let him carry me inside. Much to my surprise it was empty when we entered, there wasn't a soul to be seen.

Thank the Maker!

He carried me upstairs, and this time he actually carried me. I was almost completely out but I was awake enough to see us enter one of the larger bedrooms. He placed me on the bed. It smelled of *him*. Sweet yet woodsy. I still smelled of him from the previous night.

Please no! No more!

I took in a deep breath and felt my eyes and heart fill with stinging tears, so I let the darkness take me and carry me to a place where it hurt less.

Chapter Twenty-One

For the first time in a long time I slept without dreaming.

Thank the Maker.

The last thing I needed was to spend the night dreaming of *him* and all this madness.

I woke up still in a bit of a daze and in the middle of a very large bed with way too many covers. I fought my way to the top of the covers and took in my surroundings. It was *his* room, the one he had bought me to before. It was exactly the same except it had been removed of all evidence of him, but his presence was still here. I could smell him, feel him, and feel that he'd slept in this bed. It comforted me but killed me that little more at the same time. I finally decided to get up and face the mirror. I headed to the en-suite bathroom and found it stocked with all of my toiletries.

How do they do this?

I started to run the shower so it could warm and closed my eyes as I looked in the mirror. I slowly open them, not wanting to see the damage.

Holy Crap!

I looked incredible. I couldn't believe my eyes. I started to examine my face closer in the mirror. It was like I'd been airbrushed. My skin was flawless, my eyes sparkling and bright. My hair was thicker and shinier than before.

Crying for twenty-four hours obviously suits me.

I stopped examining my face and stepped back to examine my whole body. I was in shock. My boobs were perter, my hips curvier, and my pins looked longer and smoother than ever, and I also looked more tanned than usual, I was almost glowing.

What is going on?

I manage to pull myself away from the mirror long enough get a shower. I let the hot steamy water run over me and try to let it wash away the memories of the past few days. It has been a hell of a ride recently. Ever since the Alutiiqs came into my life.

Eli.

I couldn't help it, every time I thought of them I thought of him, every time I thought of anything I thought of him. He was locked in my mind and the worst part of all was the look on his face. All I could think about was the look on his face the last time I had seen him. It killed me. Crushed me from the inside. Every time I closed my eyes I saw it and every time I saw it my heart broke that little bit more. I wanted to spend the day in the shower pretending nothing was real, but as my dad used to say "Get up, dress up, and show up! It's the only way to show 'em who's boss, let 'em know they don't affect you," he said it to me many a times while I was starting out with The Lodge. And today felt no different. It was time to "show 'em who's boss."

I dried my hair in big loose curls hanging down my back, my auburn locks almost mirror reflective and brighter than ever. I did very light make up as I didn't seem to need it.

If I don't say so myself.

Now for the wardrobe. I threw open the large double wardrobes to see what I had to choose from and to my awe the entire thing is filled to the brim. One half were all my clothes and other were all brand-new things they must have bought for me.

Madness!

As much as I wanted to get excited and rummage through all the new expensive looking clothes I felt it best to stick with my own clothes for today. Make a stand and all that.

I start to look through my things and it's only seconds before I see my little red 1940s' number. This was my absolute favourite work outfit. It was sexy and flattering as well as being business like and professional. I loved it, and I loved me in it! Yes, this would be the outfit I would need today. Nothing says making a point like dressing like a sexy, professional bombshell to prove you're not a love stealing whore.

Oh dear!

Once ready, looking so fabulous that even Pierre would be proud, and feeling almost okay, I make my way downstairs. I hear a lot of commotion coming from the living area so I start to make my way down the hall when two giant figures come flying out of the living area and through the wall that housed the dining room. I'm knocked back a few steps with the surprise of them. They are followed out of the living area by a horde of eager bear-men looking to see what was happening. Suddenly *he* comes striding out of nowhere and picks me up.

He swoops me up into his arms and sets me down at the bottom of the stairs just in time to watch two giant men come busting through the wall and falling where I was stood only moments before. I looked from the commotion to him and back again. He didn't stop to look at me though, he was on the move instantly and grabbed the two giant men by the collar and pulled them up to standing in one swift movement. They struggled at first but once they saw who had hold of them they piped down.

"What is the meaning of this!?" he bellowed at the two men in his hands and the crowd in general. He lowered his voice "I do not expect to see this kind behaviour from a Kodiak Platoon, especially not *my* platoon!" he threw the two men he held to one side and squared himself off, he instantly had the command of the whole room. They all seemed to pull themselves to attention when he did. "I will not tolerate foul behaviour in this house or on these grounds, am I understood?"

"Yes, Sir!" they fired back.

"I understand it is Samhain and you expected leave, but things change and shit happens!" I'm hit in the gut by his choice of words and he falters for just a second.

"And I will not tolerate being disobeyed. AM I UNDERSTOOD!?" He bellowed once more.

"SIR, YES, SIR!" They bellowed back.

"Now all of you. Fix this place up before sunrise tomorrow or so help me Maker you'll pay." And with that he turned on his heels and walked out the house. I still stood not moving on the bottom step and this is the moment everyone decides to notice I'm here. They all pull up to attention, salute at me and then get on with the task at hand. Rebuilding my home.

Charlton comes rushing through the crowd towards me. "Evelyn. I'm so glad to see you up. How are you? You look…Good!" he says with an intrigued look on his face.

"I'm okay, thank you." And it was almost true. Well it was before "*Sir General Sweeps Me off My Feet a lot*" came blowing through here like a sexy tornado. I was honestly feeling kind of okay before he showed up. I almost feel it would have been easier to deal with being crushed by the two giant fighters rather than seeing him and having him save me from it all.

Maker help me!

"And how are you today?"

"Yes, I'm very well thank you," he says with a sweet, knowing smile. "I hope you found everything you needed in your room, we tried to get as much as we could on short notice."

"Short notice? What do you people do when you have time?" I laugh. He chuckles along with me, "Yes, well if we'd have known you were getting up today we'd also have finished the renovations beforehand," he says laughing but grimacing at the wreckage.

"Getting up today?" I ask a little confused. "Why would I not get up today?"

"Oh, Miss Thomas, you've been asleep for a few days, my dear. I'm so sorry, I thought you knew." He explained looking apologetic.

I just stared up at him, not really knowing what to say. "I'm so sorry. I assumed I'd just been up there overnight. Why didn't anyone wake me?"

"We just assumed you'd wake when you were ready. My apologies, Miss Thomas. We just wanted to let you rest. We checked on you regularly."

"Well, that explains the bright eyed and bushy tailed then." I say trying to lighten the mood. "So… Shall we get started then?" I ask and he looks startled. "You said we had much to discuss before. So… Shall we?"

"Well, yes, of course. If that is your wish, Miss Thomas? But are you sure you wouldn't like a little more time to process what's already happened?" he looks genuinely concerned.

"Thank you for your concern, Charlton, really, but I am honestly fine."

Oddly.

"And please, please, Charlton. Stop calling me Miss Thomas."

"Very well then, *Evelyn*. Let us begin." He said running his hands through his hair and leading the way down the hall.

Chapter Twenty-Two

One of the downstairs reception rooms had been converted into what looked like a doctor's office. It had a large sofa at one end, which is what he led us to, and a desk and filling cabinets at the other.

"Please sit," he said waving to the other end of the couch from himself. I made myself comfortable and tried to prepare myself for what was to come.

He cleared his throat and made a point of looking me right in the eyes. But it wasn't uncomfortable, it was actually very relaxing. He made me feel calm and collected. This must have been why he became a doctor. With powers like this, being a healer made perfect sense. I would easily trust him with my life, and something told me I was going to have to.

"Now, Evelyn. Some of the things we need to discuss may be distressing to you and if at any point you feel it too much or if it is something you don't wish to discuss with me, then all you have to do is say and we will stop. Okay?"

I just smile and nod.

"I need to know you understand what I'm saying to you, Evelyn? Please be sure you're ready for this before we start."

"Honestly, Charlton. I'm fine. I know I shouldn't be for so many reasons but for some other reason, today, I'm...Okay." He looks at me with what I think is pride and a little amusement.

"Well then, my dear. Let us begin."

He started off by telling me in more detail about the Succubae attack. It sounded awful. So much fighting and fear, and some very questionable, uncomfortable stories from other members of their party. But this is the nature of the succubae, they're lucky to be alive and that the succubae didn't have them killing each other instead. They had a nasty knack for making their enemies kill each other by showing them graphic hallucinations. Succubae were a nasty and dangerous bunch that shouldn't be underestimated. He then went on to tell me about Eli's arrival and the part he played. He was right. It did seem that they wouldn't have been so lucky without him. He was a true hero that morning.

My hero!

He then asked me if I wouldn't mind telling him what I had done that previous day and what had happened while Eli was with me. I was shocked that he asked and he offered to move on but I figured if it helps, then I would just have to bite the bullet and spit it out.

Not sure what difference it could make though.

So, I explained all I could remember from that day and night and made a point of being completely honest with him about my experience in the lake and with Eli. I cried a few times throughout my recollection, I just couldn't help it, the memories were painful now. He stopped me every time and offered me a tissue and to pick it up at a later date, but I insisted we carry on. Why eek out the pain, let's just rip the band aid off in one go. And it sort of helped to talk about it, to remind myself that it was actually real. And to share what happened with someone else, someone who wasn't judging me or calling me a liar. It felt good to be bonding like this with Charlton too. Once I'd finished recalling my events it was pushing 6pm and he was looking pretty beat.

"Shall we call it quits for today then?" I offered for his sake more than mine.

"If that is what you wish, my Darling, then by all means we can," he said stifling a yawn.

I giggled at him and he apologised. "I am terribly sorry. It's just been an awfully long few days. Can you forgive me?" he pleaded.

"Charlton, of course I can. You're allowed to be tired. We can't all sleep for a few days"

He just gave a short burst of laughter. "If only that were true," he said with a half-smile. "Now, would you do me the honour of joining us for dinner?" He said getting to his feet and holding out his hand for me. I had agreed and taken his hand before I thought about the possibilities of what dinner might bring.

We enter the kitchen and where the dining table used to stand was now being used as a sort of mess hall. It had canteen type tables set up, I presumed for the platoon that was now staying here. Luckily there were only a few people dotted about eating and chatting. Charlton led me over to the kitchen and opened the fridge, it was stacked high with pre-cooked food in large containers and he started to go through listing what was in there.

"The lasagne's real good today," said one of the soldiers who was washing his plate up in the sink and popping it on the draining board. "I damn near licked the plate. Sorry, Ma'am," he said suddenly remembering himself. Charlton gave him a sharp look. "What can I do you for, my dear?"

"Well, plate-licking lasagne sounds good to me." The soldier gives me a half smile-nod and leaves us.

"Lasagne it is then," Charlton said whilst serving up two portions onto plates and popping them in the microwave. "So, while you are with us, I was hoping I might be able to pester you for something? It's actually a very odd request and I totally understand if you say no…"

"Okay… What is it?"

"Will you allow me to experiment with your powers?" he says with a half grin half grimace.

"I'm sorry, you want to what?"

"It sounds much worse than it is. You see, I've never met anyone with powers quite like yours, and I assume you haven't either, so I thought it would be beyond interesting to help you tap into those powers and see what you can do?" He looked a bit lost in the excitement of it all. "This is where you run off isn't it? I'm so sorry, it was a very inappropriate question to ask, and I don't know what I was thinking?"

"I presume you were thinking it sounds like a great idea and that we should definitely do it?" he looks at me blankly, "Charlton, I think it's a great idea and we should definitely do it. I would love to know more about my powers and who better to help me?"

The biggest grin spreads across his face.

"Well this is just the best news," he beams clapping his hands together. "Ah! Brother!" he shouts into the room and I completely freeze. "Miss Thomas has agreed to let us help her with her powers. Isn't that wonderful?" he says whilst getting the lasagne out of the microwave and setting it down at the breakfast bar which I assumed was opposite Eli.

Eli!

"Will you join us for something to eat, Eli? The boys have nothing but high praise for your food."

"Your food? You cooked this? You cook?"

Of course he cooks.

Before I can think it was out of my mouth and I'm now standing directly in front of him staring up at his face.

His beautiful, beautiful face.

I blush from head to toe and I can feel my cheeks turning a deep shade of purple, but nothing matters, for those few moments we made eye contact nothing else in the world mattered at all, for those few moments it was just us.

After some time he seems to correct himself and turns to face Charlton with his hands behind his back. "Yes, this is my food, yes I cooked it and yes… I cook." He said keeping all the emotion out of his voice, he almost sounded cold. But as much as he tried to pretend, he couldn't hide from me. It must have been part of our connection. I could feel him, sense what he sensed, felt what he felt and he felt broken, just as I did. It was tearing at his insides as it was mine. This was not his doing. All this mess that had happened, it wasn't him. This was being done to him, not because of him.

It broke my heart even more to know that he was hurting too. To feel his pain was worse than carrying my own. I wanted to do everything in my power to make that pain go away for him, but I couldn't, how could I? What could I do? He had made his choice for whatever reasons and now we were both paying the price.

I went and took a seat next to Charlton and started to eat my food to try and distract myself from his radiating emotions.

"Interesting," Charlton declared out of nowhere. "Sorry, Evelyn. Please forgive me, I'll be back shortly."

"Where are you going?" I ask desperately.

"Sorry, I'll be as quick as I can. Eli, eat with Evelyn, please don't leave a lady to eat on her own." He threw over his shoulder on the way out of the room.

I suddenly feel sick with panic, I don't know if I can handle it if he sits next to me. He closes his eyes and takes a deep controlled breath and then walks round the breakfast bar, grabs the plate and sits opposite me instead.

Thank the Maker!

I sag slightly in relief, until I realise I now have to sit and look at him instead. I struggle to look up, I can't seem to draw my eyes up from the plate of lasagne.

"Am I offensive to look at or is the lasagne really that good?" he says with genuine laughter in his voice. He sounds so light hearted it makes me look up to meet his gaze. He's smiling at me.

He's smiling at me.

I feel so many things all at once. Part of me wants to leap across the table and have him right here in the kitchen and the other half wants to rip up the breakfast bar and hit him with it. But I just stare at him, open mouthed.

What a smile.

He clears his throat and loses the smile, I think realising I'm not handling it all that well.

"I'm glad to hear you're letting us help you with your powers. It should be very interesting, I look forward to it."

Excuse me?

"I'm sorry, you're looking forward to what?" I blurt out.

"Helping you with your powers?"

"I was under the impression it would just be Charlton," I say, now starting to panic slightly.

"Sorry to disappoint, but I will also be taking part in your training. Charlton needs someone for you to practise on, and there is only me." He says shrugging it off as nothing.

I feel the blood rushing to my head and I start to get dizzy. My head is starting to spin out of control. I grab my head and stumble backwards off the chair. Before I hit the floor something strong and firm is underneath me ready to catch.

I landed in his arms with a thump. My head was swirling around like a whirl pool. He placed his hands on either side of my face and brought his forehead down to meet mine.

"Evelyn, you have to focus. Do you hear me? Focus on my voice, Evelyn. Let it guide you back." I try to focus on his voice between my laboured pants. When suddenly it's only his voice I can hear and my head starts to slow. "That's it, my Little Witch, come back to me… That's it."

My head has now completely settled and I just lean against him, my breathing heavy and sweat dripping off me. His lips very lightly brush my forehead as they pass and he leans back to look at me.

"Please don't," I say wafting my hand at him. "I've had enough embarrassment to last me a lifetime, I don't need anymore."

His hand came up and very gently brushed the hair off my face and pushed it back over my shoulder. "What could you possibly have to feel embarrassed about, Evelyn Thomas?" he said with his thumb brushing my cheek and his eyes burning into me. Studying me. Searching for something. Those beautiful eyes suck me in and I am back in paradise, floating away on a sea of amber. We get lost for a moment staring at each other and suddenly he's on his feet pulling me up and propping me against the counter "Do you need any further assistants, Miss Thomas?" He says seemingly standing to attention, his whole demeanour changing, becoming cold again.

"What?" is all I can muster as tears start to sting at my eyes.

"If that is all, I will leave you to your evening?" he asks pretty much already leaving. He looks me in the eye just in time to see a loan tear run down my cheek.

Traitor!

His whole-body freezes and he just stares at me with the most pained look I have ever seen.

"Evelyn I... I can't, I'm sorry." And with that he was gone. And I was left standing on my own in the middle of the kitchen trying not to be consumed by body-shaking sobs.

Chapter Twenty-Three

The next morning, I awoke expecting to be plagued by the day before, but again I wake up in a good mood. I was starting to wonder how it was possible. I got myself ready again, this time opting for a more casual ensemble. A pair of dark green high wasted swing pants with buttons up the front, a cream billowy blouse with a deep V-neck, tucked in, and cute pair of cream pumps to match. I still looked and felt good, just toned down a bit more from yesterday. I head downstairs to see the boys have made good on their orders. The walls are as if nothing ever happened.

I'm impressed, Boys!

I head for the kitchen to see if anyone is around but it's a ghost town. I head down the corridor to see if I can find out where Charlton is but everywhere seems to be deserted. Then I hear what sounds like chanting coming from the backyard. I make my way to the back of the house and peer out the bi-folding doors that are fully open and see the most magnificent sight. A whole platoon of giant soldiers, all standing at least six and a half feet tall, dressed in nothing but combat bottoms all doing a form of Tia-Chi. The earth around then brushes up like trenches every time they changed position. It moved with them and they moved with it. Watching all of them as one with each other and the earth was a sight to behold. Steam came off their bodies in the morning mist and they seemed to have been out there for hours. They glistened in the early morning rays but one glistened in particular. He stood out. Like a beautiful dark god, in the middle of a sea of other dark gods. He was truly magnificent. He moved with such grace and elegance for a man of his size, but he was strong and commanding at the same time. He led the chant the other soldiers were repeating. I was absolutely mesmerised. So mesmerised that I didn't see Charlton arrive and lean against the door next to me.

"They're really something, aren't they? A true sight to behold."

I almost didn't hear him, I was so entranced by the man in front of me I couldn't tear my eyes off of him.

Wowzers!

"You should feel very privileged you know. There are very few people in the world he would allow to see this."

I half turn to look at him, still not able to take my eyes off Eli for longer than a second. "What do you mean? Sorry, I mean good morning, Charlton. How are you today?" feeling beyond embarrassed.

He just laughs. "This is the sacred dance of the Kodiak Bears," he says as if it should mean something to me.

"Their techniques have been held secret for generations, and Eli is one of the greatest leaders they have ever seen. He takes his role very seriously, as he does the lives of the men that serve with him," he says motioning out towards the platoon. "I've never seen him allow anyone to witness this unless it was absolutely necessary. You must mean a lot to him, Miss Thomas."

I continue to stare at him, not really hearing what Charlton has said. It takes a moment to sink in. "Mean a lot to him? HA!" I bark out, not really thinking about my surroundings. I turn back to see him looking at me while he works through the exercise, his eyes are locked on mine and they don't falter, not once. I try to look away but I can't.

He won't let me.

I continue to watch as he gracefully moves through each movement, his smooth, strong body gliding through it with perfect precision. As our eyes continue to lock his movements become even more controlled, even more precise. The ground beneath him starts to rise higher and higher with each swipe of his hand or glide of his foot. The earth working with him becomes more and more until he has no choice but to stop as it's starting to push his men away into the yard. With the size of the trenches and waves of dirt he is making he could cover this yard by himself. While the other men continue he finally stops and relaxes his body, he picks up a staff from the ground near him and starts walking over to us. Watching him walk without a shirt was intoxicating. You could see every muscle in his body move, he was like a wild animal stalking his pray from across the yard and up the porch steps.

Please let me be the prey.

He was a wild animal and right now… he looked every bit of one.

I was pretty much panting by the time he reached me. His sweat glistening body and animalistic walk nearly had me on my knees with desire. I tried to control my breathing as he closed the distance between us. I was so consumed by him I didn't even realise Charlton had left us to go sit on one of the couches in the garden room. He grabbed a towel off the porch railing and stops dead in front of me. He's so close I can smell his glorious scent. He stood directly in front of me and started to run the towel over his face. While his gaze was averted I took the opportunity to sneak a peek at him up close.

Baaaad idea!

His body was gleaming with sweat and he was beyond perfect. His giant pecks formed like boulders atop a chiselled eight pack and a gloriously defined V in his lower abdomen that disappeared into the top of his pants.

He was bronze skinned and his small patch of thick dark hair called out to me in the centre of his chest. I wanted nothing more than to reach out and run my fingers through it and then up to his thick, wet hair, round his strong neck, I wanted to pull him in to me and wrap myself around him, have his giant arms sweep me up and lock me against him.

I may have got a little carried away.

When I finally look up I find him staring down at me with hooded eyes. The heat between us is intense and almost unbearable, it had me biting my bottom lip to try and stifle a moan.

"Don't do that," he commands, pretty much breathing out the words.

"Do what?" I manage to squeeze out of my now dry throat.

His hand comes up to my face and very gently his thumbs pulls my lip out from between my teeth. "That," he answers now rubbing his thumb along my bottom lip. My breathing now laboured hitches and I have to clear my throat, this seems to bring him back to reality with a thump. He quickly drops his hand and scans the room, seeing only Charlton he relaxes somewhat but not completely. He takes a step away from me and places his hands behind his back.

What a good little soldier.

"Good morning, Miss Thomas. I trust you slept well?" he asked offering me a curt nod.

I still felt like I couldn't speak, so I just gave him a little bounce of my head in response.

"Good, now if you'll excuse me…" And he was gone again. Leaving me behind still trying to figure out where I left my brain.

I think it was somewhere around his navel…

I eventually turn and find Charlton grinning at me from the other side of the room. I take the deepest breath my lungs can muster and make my way over to him. "So, where do we start today then?" I ask trying to put the last few minutes behind me and get on with the day.

As if!

"Well, my dear, I was going to suggest we start with some power training this morning, but after that little display I think we best save that for this afternoon, wouldn't you agree?"

I cringe at the thought of someone else witnessing our "little display" just now.

"Come now, Evelyn, there's no need to worry. It's a perfectly natural process." He declares whilst jotting something down on his note pad.

"What is?" is all I can manage in response.

"Well you two, of course. I don't really know how you're keeping your hands off each other. Our mating bonds normally have us locked up in private cabins for months before we can stand to be apart from each other. But maybe it's because you haven't consummated the match yet, but give it time. It won't be long before you're a pair of wild animals going at it for days on end… My apologies." He says shaking his head and seemingly shaking off a memory. I just stare at him a bit dumbfounded. Why is he talking to me about mating rituals, especially with Eli? The look on my face must give away my thoughts.

"Dear Miss Thomas. You don't think you could pretend for too long did you? My dear girl, you two are destined… it's only a matter of time." He added a reassuring smile on the end.

"Destined? Matter of time? I don't understand." His words are confusing and hurtful. Why is he so happy to talk about us as if it's all okay? Does he not see the pain it causes me? Was he not in that hearing? Did he not hear all that was said and done to deny our bond?

I assume my face has changed again as he seems to back away slightly.

"Evelyn, my darling girl. You don't think we bought any of that crap they were peddling in Court the other day do you?" he said now resting his hands on my shoulders. "Anyone who has been in the same room as you two knows you are destined to be united, you'd have to be a fool not to have seen it from the first time you met." He said with a chuckle.

"I didn't see it," is all I can think to say.

"Well mating is a very funny thing for the people involved, especially ones who've waited so long for each other. It was magical really. I knew the first time you met each other. It was, unfortunately, a rather inappropriate first encounter, but the sparks between you two were out of this world, and the way you handled him, well… There was no doubt in my mind," he said holding on to my shoulders and grinning from ear to ear. "Pay no mind to what our elders think they can get away with. A bond like yours will not be stopped. And if I know Eli, and I do, he will find a way. He will not let you slip away now, not after all this time."

I feel a bit staggered by this new revelation from Charlton. "So, you're all aware that I didn't in fact spell him and you *know* that we are in fact mates?" I ask completely winded by the whole conversation. "So why are things the way they are if everyone knows I'm not a man stealing harpy?" I'm starting to lose my composure now and I didn't give him time to answer. "Why has any of this happened if everyone knows we are destined? Why would I be put through so much pain for no reason?" I demand, raising my voice.

"Evelyn, Evelyn, easy. I am so sorry. I assumed you knew. It was insensitive of me to talk about such things at a time like this. Please sit," he says gesturing to the couch behind us. "We apparently have much to discuss."

Over the next few hours Charlton explained in detail about what he thought had happened. He wasn't totally sure and advised me to talk to Eli if I wanted the whole story. But judging by his knowledge of his family, he didn't seem far off.

Basically, Lady Alutiiq, their Grandmother, had deemed me unsuitable for her family for whatever reason and wanted rid of me, so she's probably made Eli make some unreasonable deal that he can't refuse, involving protecting me, and same as always, she wins. He did try to assure me that it wouldn't be forever, but it all seemed a bit farfetched. Was I really that bad? Was I so far beneath them that I was unsuitable for her precious Grandson?

Screw that bitch!

I tried to let all that Charlton had said sink in, but everything still seemed so easy, rehearsed almost. Why did she have such a problem with me, and what kind of person would do this to their own Grandson? Maybe I've decided she isn't good enough for me and my family. Maybe I've decided I don't want to be associated with *her!*

How do you like them apples, Lady A?

Chapter Twenty-Four

After our little chat, Charlton requested that we take a little break while he prepares for my training this afternoon. He heads off to his study and I take a wonder round the house, it seemed pretty deserted. One or two stragglers loitering around but definitely not a full house. I head to the kitchen with the idea of getting something to eat while no one's around, but as I turn the corner I sea Eli at the stove with his back towards me. He's dressed for the day now, but still in casual combat wear. I presume for our training later.

Maker help me!

I'm trying to decide whether or not to sneak back out the room when he dangles an apron out to the side of him. "If you're going to just stand there then you can help," he says shaking the apron at me. Without hesitation I walk over and take the apron. I wasn't sure if he compelled me or I just wanted to spend time with him so badly that I jumped at the chance.

He shot my apron a look and plastered a smirk on his face.

"What?" I say looking down. It's a black apron with fluffy pink trim and a picture of a female torso in a bikini on the front.

Of course it is!

I can't help but laugh. "I think you've given me yours?" I say laughing even louder, he can't help but laugh along with me. "So, what's cooking?" I ask, giving all the pots a quick sniff. "Whatever it is, it smells incredible," I declare while my stomach rumbles.

"Are you hungry?" he asks still not looking up at me and keeping his attention on the pots.

"I am now I've smelled this." I inhale a deep breath.

Maker it smells good in here.

It's a mixture of him and incredible food.

Does it get any better?

"Grab a seat, I'll fix you something." He gestures to one of the stalls.

"Oh no, please. It's fine. I'll grab something later when you're done." My stomach growls again.

Traitor!

"Evelyn, sit and eat," he demands and I comply.

I hate that... sort of.

"What can I do you for?" he says still not looking at me but grabbing a plate and cutlery out of the cupboard.

"Um… I don't mind. What's good?"

"Excuse me? It's all good!"

"Oh, that's right. You're Mr Chef Guy as well now, aren't you? I almost forgot."

He half shoots me another smirk. "As well as what?" he says making me up a plate of food and another for himself by the looks of things.

"As well as what? Please? You're Mr Perfect are you not? I'm just waiting to find out you can fly and you'll finally be the all American Boy Scout." He's suddenly standing over me. I lean against the breakfast bar to try and put some space between us but there isn't enough room. I can't bring myself to look into his eyes again so I try and play it casual by looking elsewhere but end up looking more shifty than casual as all I can really see is his chest.

"You think I'm perfect, huh?" I can hear the smirk in his voice

"Are you not?" is all I can manage to retort.

Come on, Evie, you can do better than that!

He brings his hands either side of me and rests them on the breakfast bar behind me. He lowers his face to meet my gaze and although I try my best to avoid direct contact I fail. Miserably. I'm suddenly staring into deep amber and I am rendered unable and unwilling to fight it. I stare into him happily.

"Evelyn Thomas I am far from perfect," he says with his eyes burning into my soul "Is that okay?"

I didn't expect that.

"Is that okay?" For some reason this sparks a small rage deep inside me somewhere, or apparently not so deep. "Is that okay?" I say louder this time. "Are you freaking kidding me with this crap, *Mr Alutiiq*?" emphasising his name as they all enjoy using my full name so much. "Do you know what? No! It is not okay. None of this is okay. What part of this do you think I might be okay with? The part where I was irreversibly humiliated in front of your entire clan? Or the bit where I'm accused of being a spell wielding whore? Or maybe the part where I got my heart ripped out and shown to me while you stood back and let it happen!? OR is it the new part where I now get tortured every single day, having to be in the same room as you, being near you, smelling and feeling you everywhere I go, which damn near kills me, Eli. So please, PLEASE, tell me? WHICH PART ARE WE TALKING ABOUT, *MR*

ALUTIIQ!?" I end up shouting at him. I couldn't seem to help it.

I'm kind of emotional right now.

He looks at me as though I've stabbed him. So much pain and surprise etched in his face. "Evelyn I… I'm so sorry." He turns on his heels to leave but before I can yell at him he does a complete turn and is facing me again. His eyes are glued to the floor and he seems to be battling with something. He closes his eyes and holds the bridge of his nose for some time. Finally he takes a deep controlled breath and looks up at me again. "Evelyn. I do not know how I will ever make this right for you, but please know, please understand, that I wouldn't have done this unless there was absolutely no other choice. I did what I had to do and I would do it again. I did not make my decision lightly but it was, ultimately, the right decision. I am however sorry for the pain it has caused you, and I hope one day…" He closes his eyes and backs away from me.

"One day, what?" I ask gently.

"Never mind. I just hope you can accept my meagre apology."

"Sure," I breathe out. It's all I can muster. I feel so deflated, and a lot defeated. "This tennis match we've got going on is starting to give me whiplash, what about you?"

He just gives me a strange look.

"What do you say we make a pact? Let's leave all the drama behind and move forward."

"What's the pact?" he says flatly and looks at me with dark unreadable eyes.

"Well, no more of this, for a start. If we're… if *I'm* going to survive these close quarters then we need to be more civilised. So let's make a pact to stop all this crazy, mad, angry, sexy, tension between us and let it be a thing of the past. We have to promise to control ourselves a bit more and act more like the normal well rounded beings we were before all this nonsense started."

"If that is what you wish?" is all he says.

"Well, yes, I think it's what would be best, don't you?"

"…Sure," is now all he can muster. For a split second I see a flash of pain deep in his eyes and I regret my words instantly. I wanted to tell him that I didn't want any of this, that I wanted him to pick me up in his giant, safe arms and carry me off to some secluded nowhere so we can haul up for a few months, possibly even forever. But I couldn't. We were stuck here, still dealing with the previous decisions that were made. So for now, maybe this was for the best, because I couldn't keep being batted around like a tennis ball, never knowing which way his mood is going to swing next. "I think it would be best if we could agree to just be friends… No funny business! Just people living in the same house." I say feeling confident that I'm making the right choice. It doesn't last.

He looks at me with dark hooded eyes and slowly makes his way from across the kitchen towards where I now stood at the far end of the counter. I back up even more as he stalks me like prey. "Eli, please?" is all I can breathe out under his impenetrable stare while he closes the distance between us. I pull a chair out in front of me to try and keep some distance but he just tosses it aside like it was scrap paper. Suddenly I have no where left to back up to and I'm pressing myself up against the ceiling high cabinets hoping they might swallow me. He reaches me and just stands in front of me. Close.

Exquisitely close.

My eye level is chest height for him so I avoid his gaze for as long as I can.

"Evelyn," he growls.

I have to close my eyes to handle the way he says my name. "Please, Eli…," is all I can get out between deep, laboured breaths.

"Evelyn," he growls again "Look at me." He's not compelling me but I still can't stop myself, I look. My eyes meet his and I almost lose my knees. He must sense my weakness as a smile plays at the edge of his gorgeous lips. I so badly want to look away and run from him but I can't, every ounce of my being wants to be here with him and so much more that I can't even step to the side and put myself at a more respectable distance. I just stare achingly into his deep beautiful eyes. He leans his forearm on the cupboard behind me and brings his mouth down to my ear and whispers. "Evelyn, if you think you can control this, or ignore it, then by all means go ahead. But I, for one, know that what I feel for you is more powerful than anything I've ever known, and I don't have the strength to fight it... I don't want to fight to it. I want you more than I've ever wanted anything and I know you feel that way too. I will find a way to make this right… I just need time."

My body shaking with willpower. It is taking everything I have not to just throw myself at him and make everything right, here and now. But instead I just stand there surrounded by him, taking in deep, shaky breaths.

"You've got some self-control, I'll give you that," he says starting to pull away from me. I reach out my hand and make a fist in his t-shirt. He freezes. We've been close a bit over the last few days but there's not really been any touching.

Mm… touching.

I curl my fist tightly in the front of his t-shirt and we both watch it intently. I can feel his heart pounding in his chest. His breathing has become deep and laboured. His reaction just spurs me on. I look up to see sexy dark eyes staring down at me. Without breaking eye contact I bring up my other hand and place it on his chest and just let both my hands rest on his giant chest for a moment. I slowly run my hands up to his neck and run my fingers around his neck line then up into his hair. I glide my hands to either side of his face. With my fingers still in his hair I push my body into his. He's still completely frozen, just staring at me hungrily. I hold the position for a moment. The feeling between our bodies was sublime and I take a moment to absorb it. I can't help it, a giant smile spreads across my face. As soon as he sees it I am in the air in a flash and he hoists me onto the kitchen counter next to where we stood. My eyes quickly find his again. In an agonisingly slow motion he positions himself in between my legs and I let them wrap around his waist. Eyes locked, he very slowly dips his head to meet mine, I pull his forehead in closer and we are excruciatingly close. Ever so slowly I start to move my mouth towards his, licking my lips and biting my bottom one out of habit. He growls as I do so. "Sorry," I breathe, our lips now touching.

"Don't be," he breathes into my lips and he starts to lean closer. I lean away to play with him, stifling a giggle. Just when I'm about to give in and he slides me forward on the counter so I can't escape, a large ruckus comes from the hallway and we hear what sounds like the whole platoon coming in for lunch. Suddenly he is on the other side of the breakfast bar and I'm still sat on the counter panting with my head swirling lightly from his lack of proximity. I feel a hole return in my chest without him near me. As all the men pile into the room only one or two of them notice we're even here. I slowly slip myself off of the counter and go to leave. He blocks my path. "I thought you were helping with lunch," he says raising his eyebrows at me and smirking.

Oh boy!

I then realise I'm still wearing the apron from earlier.

Of course I am.

Chapter Twenty-Five

We spent the next hour finishing the food from earlier and getting everything ready for dinner. It felt incredible to just be near him. The hour went by as one of those long moments where everything feels perfect, and you're just happy, good old fashioned happy. There were a few sexually charged moments that weirded out some of the boys, but other than that it was all perfectly above board. And it felt wonderful.

We were nearly done cleaning up when Charlton came in. "Ah! There you both are. I'm ready when you are, although…," he said eyeing the both of us. "I haven't prepared a hose so try and control yourselves please."

I went crimson from head to toe and quickly finished what I was doing with the dishes, ditched the apron and went to follow Charlton.

"Uh-ah. Not you. You need to go upstairs and change. In the interest of science I've put something on your bed for you to wear. Although looking at him over there I wish I hadn't."

"What? Why do I need to change?"

"In order for me to monitor your progress accurately I need to monitor your body, hence… The suit." He said pointing upstairs.

"Right, I'll get changed then." I ran off as quickly as I could, like some naughty school girl who thought she got caught misbehaving.

Bad girl!

When I got to my room there was a parcel on the bed. The label read:

My Darling ~~Miss Thomas~~ *Evelyn.*

Please except my advanced apologies for the suit, it is unfortunately the only way.

Not that you've got anything to worry about.

Love and regards

Charlie

Charlie? I love it, it suits him. Now what is it with this suit?

I unwrapped the parcel on the bed and immediately saw what was wrong with the suit. It wasn't a suit. It was a second skin.

I unrolled it and tried to take it all in. It was mostly black and weighed about an ounce. It had tiny little bumps all over the surface of it and electric blue sections dotted about. I slipped my clothes off and literally slipped into the suit. It was so soft and it seemed to mould to my body once it was on. I looked down and saw that all the little bumps along the surface were now twinkling like tiny little lights and the blue parts seemed to glow, their positioning seemed to be for extra protection. It ran down the underside of the arm, down the outer thighs and calves, and then lined the sides of my waist, like a sort of armour.

I headed into the bathroom to check the damage in the full-length mirror.

Maker give me strength.

My head rolled back and I couldn't help but laugh. I've worn some form-fitting dresses in my time, but this was ridiculous. It was literally a second skin and didn't hide a single thing, it hugged tight into every single curve of my body. Luckily I'm okay with my body, not sure I'm this okay with my body with a house fool of strange bear-men, but hell, why not? I've got curves in all the right places, and I look good.

Damn good!

"Evelyn? Are you still up here? Charlie told me to fetch you." Eli yelled from the bedroom door.

"Yeah, I'm still here," I yell back.

Just.

"I'll be out in a minute."

"Okay… So, how's the suit?" I can hear the laughter in his voice.

"You jerk. You knew about this didn't you?" I say poking my head out from behind the bathroom door.

"I feel I should check the suit for you, before we head downstairs, make sure you're wearing it properly," he says strolling across the room towards me.

"No!" I raise my hand up and make a shooing motion. "You don't get to see now, you're a jerk, and jerks don't get treats."

"Treats?" his eyes lit up and he tried to open the door.

"Yes Treats! And no, I'm totally serious. You should have told me about the suit. This is not cool."

"I'm sorry, you know you don't have to wear it, you don't have to do anything you don't want to do," he said seriously but still smiling.

"I know, it's fine, you just could have given me a heads up. Now shoo!"

"You're mean!"

"If you don't leave right now I'll show you mean."

"Is that a promise?" he says smirking as he backs up out of the room.

He's such a jerk. Oh, Maker I'm in deep.

Now he's gone I start to make my way downstairs. I'm praying I don't see any of the boys on the way, but I assume they have been given strict instructions to be gone for the afternoon. There is no way he'd let them see me in this.

I reach the bi-folding doors, round off my shoulders and give my hair a good flick before sashaying my way out to meet Eli, and Charlton.

"Oh shit," Charlton blurts out when he sees me and drops his head into his hands.

Eli's head doesn't turn, he's waiting for me to get to him.

"Right," Charlton says pointing a finger at Eli. "You keep your mind on the task, do you hear me? Just… Oh for Maker's sake just get it out of your system, you've got five minutes," he says throwing his hands in the air and walking off.

I arrive next to Eli "What's his problem?" I ask looking straight ahead.

Eli turns towards me with a smile but it soon falls from his lips. He takes a moment to take me in. Opened mouthed and heavy eyed he checks over every inch of my body ending at my face and meeting my eyes.

Watching him admire and desire my body in such a way was empowering. It made me feel incredible, but it also made me so incredibly hot for him.

We stared at each other for some time, he flinched every now and then as though he was going to move but he didn't. It seemed to be taking everything he had not to come for me, he was grinding his jaw so hard I could hear it from a few feet away. Seeing him so affected by the suit gave me a weird sense of power. I decided to have some fun with him.

I looked at his lips for a moment and then slipped my bottom lip between my teeth. I could hear him growling in front of me. I then turned to the side slightly and let my hands run slowly down my leg until I reached my shoe, I made a minor adjustment before slowly rising back up. When I met his gaze again he seemed to have acquired a dark gleam to his eyes and a half smile playing at the edge of his lips. He raised his eyebrows at me. "So you want to play with me, huh?" he says closing the gap between us in two easy strides. He stands as close to me as he can get and leans his face down so he can look into my eyes. "Huh?" he says bumping his nose on mine.

I look down to the ground for a moment then flick my eyes up to meet his, with my bottom lip between my teeth. I bring my mouth up to his ear so my lips are touching him "Yeah I do. Is that okay?"

He throws his head back with a deep dirty chuckle that quickly turns into a growl. He suddenly has me up in the air and I'm wrapping my legs around his waist. He sets me down on the porch ledge and leans into me.

Oh, Maker he feels amazing between my thighs.

"This is about where we left off earlier was it not?" he asks leaning his forehead against mine.

"Almost," I say shifting myself forward into his pelvis and running my fingers further into his hair, gripping it at the back. "I think this is better."

"Yes it is," he says running his nose and lips up my neck to behind my ear and inhaling deeply. "Yes. It. Is." He says in my ear before coming back to rest his forehead on mine. Just when I think we're going to explode with passion he pulls his head back and finds my eyes. He grabs both sides of my face and slowly lowers his lips to mine, he just brushes them against mine when Charlton returns. Within a beat he's gone and the hole finds its way back into my chest. I slide myself off the porch and head to where Charlton is setting up.

"As much as I hate to stand in the way of young love, we must press on, and you two nearly blew up my equipment with whatever you were doing, no more of that in the suit, it can't handle the both of you."

I dare to sneak a side glance at Eli, he's standing just off to the left of me staring intently at Charlton. But he is also completely rigid and grinding his back teeth again. I can't help but smile to myself.

Ha-ha! I did that!

I expected Charlton to have a lot of machinery hooked up, but he had nothing but a large tablet he held in one hand. He sat in one of the garden armchairs and looked up at me expectantly. "So, shall we begin?" he said with a big grin on his face.

"Sure, let's do this."

"Right, so what do we already know you can do? Other than the basics."

"Okay, I have telekinesis, so I can move almost all objects at will, I can also move people when necessary." I feel a slight wave of embarrassment as Eli shifts next to me, remembering I have done it to him before. "I can control elements, when they allow it…Um…"

"What does that mean? When they allow it?" Charlton asks whist making notes on his tablet.

"Well, they have their own personality, it's never the same twice with elements. They're unpredictable. So… When they allow it, I can control them, but I can always harness them, who's in control just varies."

He looks at me intently and then goes back to making notes and waves his hand as if for me to carry on.

"Um… I can read emotions. I can predict the weather…"

"I'm sorry, you can predict the weather?" he asks looking at me with mild shock.

"Yeah, so I know what the weather will be like. Only like, a while before it happens. I can't tell what it will be like next week or anything."

"She can also teleport," Eli added.

"And yeah, I've teleported twice now."

"Have you? That's a very unusual ability these days," he says eagerly making notes on his tablet. "Well that's great. Can we work on that first?"

"Teleporting? Um yeah, sure. What do you want me to do?"

"Well, let's start with short distances, shall we? Pick a spot in the garden and try and teleport there."

I picked a random spot in the garden and concentrated solely on the spot, or so I thought. I felt the semi-familiar pull of teleporting but I opened my eyes I'd ended up popping up right in the spot where Eli stood, I ended up so close to him he toppled over backwards and took me with him.

Quickly getting myself up and trying to hide my embarrassment, I head back to where I'd started and try again. All the while Charlton was making notes on his tablet.

This time I really focused on the spot, and nothing else, I envisage myself standing in the spot and waving back at them. Next thing I know I feel the pull, open my eyes and there I am, waving back at them from the other side of the yard.

"Now come back," yells Charlton

So, I do the same as before, but this time I managed to get a bit too close to Eli again and he nearly jumps out of his skin.

We worked on teleporting for about an hour, I got further and further away each time, but we didn't go further than the County line, we didn't want to risk going too far today.

Although I felt that was far enough.

Every now and then I would get a bit closer to Eli than I was supposed to but I didn't knock him over again, so not all bad.

"Can I propose an experiment?"

I nod in reply.

"Can we see if you can teleport to Eli?"

"*To* him? What does that mean?"

"So, Eli will stand somewhere in the garden and you'll try and teleport to him without knowing where he is standing. Clear?"

"Yeah, I think so."

Eli walks off behind me and I wait for Charlton to tell me when he's ready.

"Okay, Evie. Whenever you're ready."

This time I try and get the teleporting feeling beforehand. Once I start to feel a pull I think only of Eli and I pop up right in front of him, so close that my nose is touching his t-shirt. I look up and he is smiling down at me. "Hi," he growls with a smirk.

"Wow, Evelyn that really is fascinating. You seem to have a direct pull to Eli, even given the fact that you two are to be united, it's still very unusual… Interesting, very interesting," he said walking off making notes on his tablet. "Talk amongst yourselves, I won't be a moment," he threw over his shoulder.

Eli's eyes locked with mine, "Do we have to talk? We've done enough talking for one day," he growled whilst rubbing my nose with his. His arms came up around my sides and his hands found my hips. "This is a hell of a suit, Miss Thomas, it doesn't leave very much to imagination though, does it?" he said eyeing me up and down whilst turning my hips with his hands. His touch was burning even through the suit, maybe even more so in the suit. I seemed to feel more in tune with my senses in it and he was invading all of them. His smell, his eyes, his touch, his taste.

Oh, Maker I need to taste him again.

I needed to feel his lips on mine, his flesh on my flesh.

Take it easy, Evelyn.

His hot hands engulfed my waist and hips, I was tiny in his grip. His arms wrapped around me and pulled me in to him, I responded by putting my arms around his neck and my hands in is hair. I had to go up on tiptoes a bit so I could reach better, and he had to support my weight, but that just made it sexier.

"Evelyn Thomas… You do some serious things to me. Do you know that?" he whispered in my ear, it was barely audible, but even without him saying a word, I knew how he felt. His emotions were radiating off of him and I welcomed them. They matched my own entirely. What we felt, we felt together. There was no denying it. The more time we spent together, the more in-tune we were becoming.

"Do you have plans for tonight?" he asks brushing some stray hair out of my face.

"Um… yeah, yeah I do, sorry," I say playing with him and giving him an awkward sorry face.

"Oh really? And what might they be?" he says leaning his head down and putting his lips to my ear. "I know what I'd like them to be," he puts my earlobe between his teeth and pulls slightly then plants a row of tiny soft kisses down my neck.

I try to keep playing with him, but my body isn't joining in. His touch fires electricity all over me and it responds to him with or without my say so. "Yeah, um… I have a date," I breathe out between laboured breaths. His grip tightens on my words. "Oh you do huh? Who with, might I ask?" he puts his right hand at the back of my head and in my hair so he can roll my head round to the other side and repeat his torture of tiny kisses on the other side of my neck.

"Just one of the boys. We got to talking about lasagne, you know… One thing leads to another…" Suddenly I'm in the air again with my legs wrapping round his hips and with lightning speed he takes us to the other side of the yard and out of Charlton's eye line. He leans me up against a tree and looks deep into my eyes. "You seem to be playing with me a lot today, Miss Thomas."

"Who said I was playing?" I give him the most innocent look I can muster and a deep growl comes from deep within him.

"You know, I was going to let you get away with it because you're cute, but now I'm thinking that it would be much more fun to join in." He has the darkest, sexiest look in his eyes, it sends a thrill up my spine and electricity everywhere else.

"You wanna play? We can play." Instantly his eyes are smouldering at me, burning with so much desire it feels like my heart stops and everything becomes serious. He lifts me a little higher onto his hips and pushes into me a bit more. I can feel his excitement pushing up against my pelvis and it sends a fire throughout my body. I tighten my legs around him to draw him even closer and he doesn't fight me. He starts by gliding his hands excruciatingly slowly up my thighs, the grips me tightly and rocks slightly when he reaches my hips.

Maker, it's exquisite!

He then ever so slowly pushes his hands up the sides of my waist, brushing his thumbs over the curve of my breast as he gets there. Then they move round to my back. He pulls me into him as tightly as he can, wraps one hand around my waist and other goes to the back of my head and into my hair. My body is his, I have no fight to give him, and I don't want to. I want him to take me, here, now, and any way he wants to. I've never belonged to anyone more. He leans his head down, lightly rubs his nose against mine and brushes my lips with his, he pauses for the longest moment… Just long enough so that all that is left of me can become consumed by him. He runs his nose along my jaw line and stops when his lips meet my ear. "Enjoy your date, Miss Thomas." Then he was gone and I was left leaning up against the tree, panting and doubled over, and he was gone.

Sexy jerk!

Chapter Twenty-Six

We spent the next few hours working on the teleporting, trying to speed up the process. Charlton wanted me to be able to zap in and out of different spaces at lightning speed, I assumed it wold be used as a combat technique. No idea what I would ever need that for but it was fun so I played along. Within an hour or so I was zapping here there and everywhere perfectly, and still managing to give Eli the cold shoulder for his performance earlier. I wasn't really mad at him, if him being maddeningly sexy was his idea of playing with me then so be it, however it did leave me aggravatingly turned on with no outlet, so I figure he deserved to sweat a little.

"Right, let's call it there for today, shall we?" Charlton declared flopping into the armchair again. "I don't know about you, but I'm beat." He popped his tablet down on the table for the first time since we got out here. "I have one last thing I'd like to try. Eli, go somewhere inside the house anywhere at all, and Evelyn, dear, try and teleport to where he is."

"Why is that different from before?" Eli asks.

"I just wanted to see if being confined by walls made a difference. Eli, let me know how it goes later." and with that Eli was gone.

"Right, my dear. Whenever you're ready."

I concentrated on nothing but Eli. I saw him in my head and felt the normal pull and pop. But this time I landed horizontally lying on my front and on top of him.

"Well done," he said grinning up at me looking really pleased with himself. I went to push myself off of him and get up but he held on to me tightly. "Where are you rushing off too?" He said searching my eyes. I think checking to see if I was really pissed at him. Of course I wasn't, but he didn't need to know that just yet. So I just gave him a hard stare, unfortunately it didn't have the desired effect, he just laughed at me. It was such a big laugh filled with so much boyish charm I couldn't help but give in to him. My face lit up at the sight of him belly laughing under me, I was grinning from ear to ear. As soon as he saw me smiling his laughing calmed and he cupped my face in his hands. "That is the most beautiful sight I have ever seen," he says whilst taking in every inch of my face.

"You're not so bad yourself," is all I think to reply with. He starts laughing again.

When I eventually try and get up so I can get out of this suit he stops me again. "Where are you going?" he almost looks worried.

I give him a soft smile, "Just to change out of this suit," I say as I turn round and fling my feet out of the bed. The suit still has me slightly buzzed I think, I have a serious bounce in my step.

Although that could be due to my new friend in the bed there.

I go over to the closet and grab out some sweats and my favourite Tee and head for the bathroom.

"Boo! Where's the floor show?" he shouts from the bed. He's now on his back resting on his elbows. He shoots me a wink and a dazzling smile.

Oh, that's going to get me trouble.

Once in the privacy of the bathroom I peel the skin-tight suit off my body and jump in the shower, only a quick rinse to wash the day off of me before bed. I throw on my sweats and Tee and head back out into the bedroom. He was gone. I instantly felt the hole in my chest creeping back until I saw a plate and a note on the bed.

Evie,

Have a few things to do this evening, but was

hoping I could see you after your date?

I fixed you something to eat.

Eat it! And get some rest.

See you at 9.

Eli

I check the bedside clock, 19:03, only two hours to wait.

It was going to feel like forever!

I decide some time to relax might be nice. I grab the plate, head out onto the balcony and get comfy in one of the armchairs out there, it's a bit chilly so I wrap myself in one of the blankets and decide to see what I've got for dinner.

It was a giant stack of pancakes. There were at least five of them and they were dripping with syrup. My eyes lit up. I dug the fork in and shoved a massive slice of pancake into my mouth and some syrup dripped down my chin. They were the fluffiest lightest cakes I'd ever eaten, and then came the peanut butter.

Maker bless you! Peanut butter pancakes, how did he know?

Peanut butter pancakes would be my desert island food. My two favourite things combined. I stuff in another massive mouthful and suddenly I hear cheering coming from below. I look towards the garden and see about fifteen of the boys looking up at me cheering and laughing.

For Maker's sake!

I chomp down on my mouthful and give them a mock regal wave. In unison they elaborately bow at me and finally walk off laughing and joking.

They all looked fairly well dressed, there must be an event tonight. Samhain must go on I guess. I can't for the life of me remember what it is. I've only been out of the loop for nearly a week now and I'm already losing my edge.

I chomp down mouthfuls of perfect peanut butter pancake until I've had my fill and then I decide a bath would be nice. I felt like I needed to do something normal.

I popped the lid back over what was left of the stack and started to run a bath. They'd kitted the bathroom out with spa like toiletries so I grabbed a handful and filled the bath with all sorts of wonderful smells and luxurious creams. I grabbed what I thought was a night shirt out of one of the draws in the dresser, but when I unfolded it, it was one of Eli's shirts. His smell radiated off of it.

Perfect!

I slipped into the bath and just let the bubbles and hot water relax me while the steam filled the room. I tried not to think of anything but my mind was stuck on one thing.

Eli.

I tried everything I could to not think of him, but it always came back to my beautiful bear-man. I thought of how incredibly passionate this day had been, and how wonderful it had been to be with him. We hadn't even kissed today but the heat between us had been exquisite, excruciating, but exquisite none the less. The look on his

face when he saw me in the suit played in my memory
over and over, it gave me such power. And the way his
eyes get dark and a smile plays around his lips when he's
turned on.

*Oh Maker, I want to spend the rest of my life on the end of
that look.*

After I waste some more time soaking up the bubbles
and thinking of my sexy bear I figure it must be nearly
time. I quickly get out of the bath and dry my hair off a bit
and just let my long loose curls hang down my back. I slip
his oversized shirt on and head into the bedroom. 21:09,
he'll be here soon. I head out to the balcony and get some
fresh air to wake me up a bit after my bath. It's a beautiful
night. I let my hair blow around me in the strong breeze
and take a few deep breaths of the night air.

It smells like autumn.

Prefect!

Then I get another smell. Eli.

I turn round to see the giant Adonis standing behind
me, leaning up against the doorframe to the bedroom with
a sexy smile and hooded dark eyes.

"Good evening, Miss Thomas," he says smirking at me.

"Hi," is all I can manage. I feel like I need to hold onto
the railing to stay standing. Watching him in the

moonlight, like this, with that smile on his face, nearly floored me. I want him more than anything.

The wind starts to pick up a bit and send a chill up my spine and my hair flying around my face. He holds out a hand to me "Come, let's get you in the warm."

"But there's such a great view out here," I say smirking at him.

"Well I can't argue with that, Miss Thomas," he says striding across the balcony and stopping right in front of me. "The view is spectacular." He grabs my hips and pulls me into him. "But aren't you cold?"

"Not anymore," I say sliding my arms around him and hugging into his chest. He wraps his arms around me and picks me up. We move a few feet and he sits us down in one of the armchairs. I curl up in his lap and nuzzle into his neck. It almost feels like he doesn't know what to do, like he's uncomfortable or something. I lean my head back and look at him. "Are you okay? Do you want me to move?"

"Move? No! I want you to stay there for ever." His voice was low and sexy. He lifts his hands to either side of my face and pulls me into him. His lips gently brush mine and he just holds me there for a moment "Evelyn," he breathes. "We really need to talk."

I can't even think about what he's said or has to say, all day I've been waiting for this kiss. Over two hundred years I've been waiting for this kiss, and it was happening now. I put my knees either side of him on the chair and leaned my body up against him, all the while we were still lips to lips. I run my hands around his shoulders and brought them up to his neck and hairline. I rubbed my nose on his "No more talking," I breathed and he drew me into him and our lips met, properly this time. We kissed each other with everything we had. It started off strong and impatient but slowly settled and became hot, slow and sexy. His hands found every part of me while his lips hypnotised me into a solitary state of arousal. It felt primal, it felt right.

In this moment I felt like he was the only other person on the planet and we could stay like this forever.

After a while things were reaching dangerous levels of hot. The kisses had become fevered again and I was now tugging at his clothes. He slid his hands down my back and under my ass. He hoisted himself and me up and strode back into the bedroom and put me down on the end of the bed. He lifted his shirt over his head and kneeled on the floor in front of me. It made us equal head height. His eyes were so dark in the moonlight and his face showed only one thing. Desire.

He pulled me up against him and wrapped my legs around his waist. I put my arms around his neck and let my fingers find his hair. He bought his hands up and pulled my face towards him and into a deep slow kiss. After a while I pulled back and bit his lip lightly with my teeth. A low growl rumbled in his chest and it spurred me on. I placed a line of tiny kisses along his jaw up to his ear, I take his earlobe in my teeth and let out a half moan half breath. The growl gets louder and so do his emotions. No one has ever wanted me the way he does right now, and I've never wanted anyone the way I do him. I trace another line of soft kisses down his neck and then pull away from him and start to slide myself back further onto the bed, my legs slide between his hands as I go. Once I stop he starts to move towards me. The muscle in his back and shoulders are like that of an animal. He crawls onto the bed and works his way up my body. He reaches my thighs and parts my legs with his knee. He grabs my thighs and pulls me towards him, then lowers himself onto his hands either side of me. I stare up into his eyes and I'm gone. I reach up and pull him into me, crushing his lips against mine. I wrap my legs around him so our bodies are flush and I can feel all of him against me. My hands are gripping in his hair and his are roaming my body. Just as I think this is going to the next level he is gone. Off me in a beat and standing on the other side of the room. I'm left lying on the bed panting and pissed. It takes me a few minutes to gather myself but eventually I get up to look for him. He was out on the balcony leaning his forearms against the railings. I was somewhat pissed at him still but I couldn't deny what a sight he was out there in the moonlight glistening like the Adonis he was. I took a moment to take him in, then made my way over to him. I just stand next to him staring out into the night.

"Hey." I sneak in a side glance and his face is pained with worry. There were so many emotions coming off of him I didn't know which one to focus on.

"Eli, are you okay?" I ask getting worried now. I rest my hand on his shoulder and he instantly drops to his knees and rests his head on my stomach. I put my hands on his shoulders and lower myself down with him. "Eli? You're kinda' freaking me out. What's going on?"

He finally looks up and meets my eyes. "I'm so sorry, Evelyn. I came here tonight to talk to you. I never meant for all this to happen. I just couldn't control myself. Once I saw you standing out here under the moonlight in my shirt… I was lost to you. I'm so sorry."

"Wait, what is it you're sorry for? I don't understand."

"There are thing you need to know before this goes any further. Things that may determine whether or not this goes any further."

"What does that mean?" I can feel panic rising in my throat.

He pulls me to my feet and leads me back into the bedroom but this time to the armchairs by the fire place. He pushes a button on the side of the fire and it roars to life. He passes me a blanket and sits in the chair opposite me.

"Evelyn… The deal I made with my grandmother was simple enough. I pretend that what we have isn't real, and testify to that in court and in return she would allow us to do what was necessary to keep you safe. But the one thing you can always count on with my grandmother, is there's always a catch." He adjusts himself in the chair so he is no longer facing me and now looks into the flames instead. "The catch was that I am now seemly single and without a mate…" He takes a moment. "She has recently agreed to a treaty between our clan and another rival clan from England. The treaty will be sealed with a union of a high council member from each clan."

My blood runs cold.

Please don't say it.

"And that member will be me."

And there it is.

He finishes up by telling me that it's a very common practise amongst his people and she's done it a few times to varying members. Including Charlton.

What? Charlton is married... what?

And then he just sits there in silence staring at the flames, seemingly waiting for me to say something. But I don't know what to say. I sit there staring at him for some time when he finally looks at me, "Please, Evelyn, say something, anything. I need to know what you're thinking."

"I don't really know what I'm thinking, Eli… You're engaged? What am I supposed to be thinking?"

"I am not engaged, Evelyn! You make it sound like I proposed to someone. This is nothing more than a political move that my grandmother is making. I don't even know this woman."

At the mention of the other woman my blood starts to boil. I can feel a green-eyed rage stirring in the pit of my stomach and his eyes widen at me. "Evelyn, are you okay?" He says cautiously.

"Not really, Eli, no!" he looks scared. "And you looking at me like that isn't helping!"

"You need to take a look in the mirror," he says getting up and offering me a hand. I ignore his hand and get up and march over to the mirror on the dresser.

Mother Maker! What the…?

My eyes are glowing a bright white-blue and the whites are glowing slightly too. I look at myself in the mirror with my mouth hanging open. I've never seen anything like this, on me or anyone else. As I start to calm they start to fade.

"What *was* that?" I ask no one in particular.

"I've never seen anything like that before. I have no idea."

I check my eyes closely in the mirror one last time before heading out onto the balcony.

I lean against the railings and he hangs back by the door. I try my best to make sense of all this, but I can't. I turn to face him.

"So… What do we do now?"

"I can't answer that, Evelyn. It has to be your decision."

"Oh what crap! How is it my decision? None of this has anything to do with me. This is all you." I throw at him as I storm past him back into the bedroom.

"I am killing myself trying to fix this, Evelyn. I don't know what more I can do."

"Um… Say no!? How about that?"

"I can't. If I say no then there's no one to protect you."

"If you say yes, there's no me to protect!" I yell at him.

"What do you mean?" he say walking up to me. "Evelyn? What do you mean?" He grabs my shoulders and makes me look at him.

"There is no power on this earth that would keep me here to watch you marry another woman, Eli!" I try to keep my voice from wavering but it's no use, my eyes are starting to sting with tears.

"Evelyn, it's really not how you think. Its only paper. Charlton sees his wife twice a year at clan gatherings. That's it."

"So to your clan you would be married to her, and I… I would be what? Huh? Eli? What would I be?" He doesn't answer. "Your mistress? Your bit on the side? Your whore? Huh? Which one, Eli? Which one am I?" I shrug him off my shoulders and go to walk away but he grabs my arm.

"My life, Evelyn. You would be my life."

Shit!

I flop on the edge of the bed and run my fingers though my hair, letting out a deep sigh and trying my hardest not to cry.

"Evelyn," he says kneeling in front of me. "Please give me a chance to fix this? I promise you I am trying. I promise you I am doing everything in my power to fix this, I just need time." I look into his eyes and he looks so pained, so much stress etched into this gorgeous features.

"I can't watch you marry another woman, Eli. That's the only thing I can promise you right now." And with that the tears come. They roll down my face in an uncontrollable stream and I feel the sobs building in the pit of my stomach. He scoops me up into his arms and lays us both down on the bed. He sets my head on his chest and holds me tight while I cry. Every now and then he kisses the top of my head and tells me everything is going to be okay. And I really needed to believe that. It had been a real crazy few weeks and I needed to believe all would get better.

Chapter Twenty-Seven

I must have drifted off to sleep at some point as I woke a few hours later curled up in a mound of bed covers and pillows. I searched the bed for him but he wasn't there. I lay there for little while looking up at the canopy over the bed when he comes back into the room with a tray of drinks and food.

"Hey, sorry. I didn't want you to wake up on your own, but I thought you'd need something when you did. Can I get you anything?"

I just shake my head no. But then I smell the food... Peanut butter pancakes.

"Are they the same pancakes as earlier?" I ask, my voice hoarse and harsh.

"Yes, Batman." He says mimicking a Batman voice to mock me.

"You really think you can get away with mocking me right now?" I raise my eyebrows at him.

"Yes they're the ones from earlier, why?"

"Because they're the best thing I ever put in my mouth, that's why."

He gives me a sexy smirk while handing me a plate of stacks. I roll my eyes at him and take the stacks.

"So you like my stacks, huh?"

I shovel a massive mouthful into my mouth. "You could say that, yeah."

"What would you say?" He says laughing at me.

I swallow down the mouthful with difficulty. "Oh Maker! I love these pancakes!" I yell. He rolls his head back and laughs.

I love making him do that.

"It's like they were made for me. My two favourite foods shoved together in one glorious mess! Yes!" we both laugh and I shovel in another mouthful.

We both tuck into our stacks until we're full and then a weird awkwardness falls over us. We don't know how we're supposed to be now. We just sit on the bed, not talking, not moving, and avoiding eye contact.

I know if I looked into those eyes I'd be lost again, and judging by earlier, that could be dangerous. I didn't want to get into anything before I knew where we stood.

He seemed to read my mind and turned to face me, "Evelyn, I need you to know that the last twenty four hours have been the best of my life. I never realised I was waiting for you to find me, I never realised there was a part of me missing. But now I know I've waited forever for you and now that I have y-… Now that you're here… I never want to be without you again."

And there goes my resolve.

My eyes start to sting with tears again and I can't help but get lost looking in his eyes. I want him to scoop me up and take me away from here, far away. But he doesn't move. He just sits there, frozen, waiting for me to let him know it's okay.

He finally turns his head away from me and his body seems to sag over. I slowly move towards him and end up knelt next to him on the bed. He turns to look at me a little taken back. A few stray tears roll down my cheeks and he watches them fall. "Evelyn, I…"

I put my fingers on his lips. "Eli, there is only one thing I need to know, and I already know it." I put my hands in his hair and pulled him into me for a gentle kiss. It takes him a moment to respond, as if he can't believe what is happening. But he quickly corrects himself and wraps his arms around me and pulls me onto his lap. I straddle his legs and he ups the ante on the kiss. It's now slow and sensual and pulls me further and further under his spell. After a while I pull back, a little light headed and swooning big time, I go to move off of him but he stops me.

"What's wrong? Are you okay?"

"Calm yourself, Big boy. I'm just getting a drink." I grab one of the water bottles he brought up earlier and guzzle down half and offered him the rest. He takes the bottle and my hand and pulls me back over to him. "Big boy?" he asks with a smirk.

"Yeah, well…I'm hoping, you know?" I say winking at him. He just laughs and pulls me further into him so I'm now standing between his legs while he sits on the edge of the bed.

"It's late," he says checking the clock on the night stand. "We should get you to bed."

I instinctively pull my bottom lip between my teeth and he lets off a low growl. The idea of him getting me to bed only results in a one thought process for me.

He stands up in front of me and brings his hands to my face. He pulls my lip from between my teeth and runs his thumbs along my cheeks, putting his fingers through my hair and round the back of my neck he leans in and gives me the gentlest kiss. He brushes his lips on mine and breathes "Not tonight, my Little Witch. I want everything to be perfect first."

"First?"

"Before you find out if I can keep the big boy nickname." He adds a wink to the end and kisses me again.

After he's finished his sexy, tender assault on my lips and my knees feel like they might buckle, he swoops me up in his arms and places me gently on the bed, with my head on the pillows. He climbs in next to me and pulls me up onto his chest. He runs one hand through my hair and the other plays with my fingers. It feels like no time at all before I'm drifting off into a deep sleep and dreaming of bears, cubs and evil succubae.

I wake the next morning feeling completely revitalised and refreshed, which is odd considering we were up till 3am and its now only 7am. I decide to let myself lay there a little longer and think about the previous night when giant arms wrap themselves around me and pull me in to a strong, warm embrace. I curl up in his arms and enjoy the warmth of him. I eventually look up and find his eyes. They're dark, hooded and sleepy and they light all kinds of fires inside me. I can't help myself. I pull myself up so we're face to face and nudge his nose with mine. He's just smiling at me through his dark, sexy morning face, "Good morning," he grins.

I respond by pushing myself into him and letting our lips meet with a good strong kiss. His body responds without hesitation. Wrapping ourselves around each other we spend nearly an hour saying good morning.

Eventually he pulls away declaring we have to get up and ready for the day ahead. I lay in the bed moaning about the distance between us while I watch him start to get ready. He loses the sweatpants he was wearing for bed and struts around gathering his things in his underpants. They're jet black shorts that hang low on his hips, allowing full view of his exquisite torso and showing me more of that sexy V that finishes below the hem of his shorts.

Maker I want to see where that ends.

And as if reading my mind he stands in front of the bathroom door, drops his shorts, flings them at me and disappears into the bathroom.

"Boo! Where's the floor show?" I yell at him.

Deciding to finally get up myself, I make my way over to the closet to pick out something to wear for the day. I make a mental note to ask Charlton for a schedule so I know what we're doing each day, as picking outfits was becoming tricky. I felt good today, the best I'd ever felt actually, so I wanted to look good too. I decided on a calf length black pencil skirt and a beige, long sleeved top, with a very low V-neck. I slipped his shirt off and wearing nothing else I slip on a short silk dressing gown. As he comes back into the room I try to cover myself up but there's no belt on the gown so it hangs open revealing some of my breasts and tiny black briefs.

I want him to see me like this.

He walks over to the dresser and pulls out a few things without looking at me. "I have a few things to do this morning, but I'll see you for training this afternoo…" he looks over to me, drops everything he's holding and with two giant strides he has me in the air, legs around his waist and his arms crushing me into him. He pushes me up against the wall and consumes me with a hot passionate kiss.

Once again I am lost in him, praying that this will be the time he finishes what he's started and devours me completely. But after a few insanely hot minutes, he pulls back and lowers me to the floor. I have to use the wall for support as my legs have turned to jelly. With his head leaning down on mine he kisses the top of it and rests his hands on my hips. "I have to go," he breathes.

"Well… Then you're stupid," I manage to get out between laboured breaths.

"I am stupid." He runs his lips up and down my neck. "So, very stupid." He gives me one last firm kiss on the lips, turns on his heels and heads for the door. He turns to me just before he leaves with the biggest, sexiest smile on his face. "Have a good day, my Little Witch." And he's gone.

Chapter Twenty-Eight

Once dressed and ready I make my way downstairs to find the entrance hall full of people. From what I can make out it's the platoon, but why they're gathered in here I don't know. I try and peer past them to see what all the fuss is about when they suddenly all start to disperse frantically. And that's when I hear her.

Lady A!

I panic slightly at the thought of seeing her, I frantically scan the area for somewhere to hide but the closest place is a few feet away, she would catch me be before I made it that far. Suddenly there is a wall of men in front of me and one of them I recognised was ducking behind the rest signalling for me to follow. I duck behind them and follow as instructed. I get half way down the line of men and she enters the entrance hall. We both freeze.

"Charlton I don't care what you say, it looks bad for him to be living in this house with *her*."

I know it's me she's talking about, I can tell by the distain in her voice, that and I'm the only female staying in the house.

"He should be staying in his room as intended. As should you!"

I can't see her face but I can imagine the look she is giving him. I can feel myself getting riled up by her presence and attitude, but just as I feel myself start to boil a gentle hand rests on my shoulder. I now notice it's the lasagne guy from the kitchen last week. He meets my gaze with a smile and then places a finger over his lips to shush me. Seeing the pleading in his eyes calms me immediately. She wouldn't just find me back here after all.

She and Charlton start to head for the kitchen and lasagne boy starts to lead me further down the hall, he suddenly stops short and rises to full height and attention.

"Sir." He salutes

"What in the Maker's names is going on here, Lieutenant?"

"Sir! Lady Alutiiq has arrived for a visit, Sir!"

"I fail to see why that has you crawling around like an idiot, Lieutenant Harper?"

"Eli, is that you?" Lady Alutiiq calls. "What's all this noise out here?"

I try to get his attention but he is looking in her direction now and if I move she'll see me. I start to panic again. I'm not overly fussed about seeing her but it would look ridiculous on my part if I'd tried to hide from her in such a way.

"Ah, Lady Alanjula. What brings you out here?" he asks holding out a hand to greet her.

*"**No, idiot**!"* I think to myself.

"What?" he replies out loud.

My heart stops.

Is he answering me?

"What? What are you what'ing at, Boy?"

"Sorry, Ma'am. I thought you said something." He starts to subtly look around.

I concentrate as hard as I can and focus on only him. *"**Eli**? **Can you hear me**?"*

*"**What's happening**?"* he thinks.

*"**It's only me. I'm so sorry. I'm behind Harper. He was trying to sneak me out of here when you showed up.**"*

"How are you doing this?" he says out loud.

"Doing what, Eli?" says Lady A with an annoyed tone to her voice. "What is it you keep blithering about boy?"

"Err, nothing Ma'am. Please forgive me, it's been a long week."

"Just like your father! Always blithering about something. You need to learn to control yourself, Boy. You don't want to end up like him do you? A blithering idiot, banished for being so."

Something makes me want to jump up and start defending him but the same gentle hand touches my shoulder and calms me again. I look up at him but he is still at attention, stood stock still and eyes front, with just one stray hand resting on my shoulder.

"Eli, please, get her out of here."

"No, Ma'am, I certainly wouldn't. Shall we take some tea in the kitchen?"

"Well that is where Charlton was taking me before your interruption." She says walking off. "You may join us… if you insist."

What a bitch!

"Please, Ma'am. I will escort you then be on my way."

"Highly unnecessary. Be gone with you. All of you in fact," she says eyeing the line-up. "Why are you all loitering around here? Don't you have anything better to do?"

"MA'AM, YES, MA'AM!" They all shout in response and salute in unison, making Lady A nearly jump out of her skin.

"For Maker's sake!" she says clutching her chest over-dramatically. "Be gone with you. Now!" she demands.

We all file out of the hallway and through to the garden room. I manage to go unnoticed by keeping in between Harper and a few of the others.

Once in the garden room I start to relax.

"Where is she?" I hear him ask and the crowd splits. I stand there looking sheepish and blushing from head to toe. I feel like a complete idiot and I'm pretty sure he's going to tell me so, until he starts laughing that is. He rolls his head back and lets out a full belly laugh. The men around us start to filter off, I quickly grab the arm of Lieutenant Harper before he can leave.

"Thank you!" I say looking up at him.

"Please, Ma'am, it's no trouble," he says giving me a nod and a second one to Eli.

"It could have been, though. Easily. So thank you. And please, call me Evelyn," I say releasing him and smiling. He looks over to Eli as if to check if it's okay. He nods.

"Don't be checking with him. I make my own decisions, thank you very much."

"Understood, Ma'am, but I don't," he says winking at me and turning to leave.

"Lieutenant Harper," Eli calls

"Sir!" he replies, saluting at the same time.

"Pass on to the rest of the boys that tonight is a freebie. Once routine is finished the night is yours. But I want everyone back here by sunrise, is that understood?"

"Sir, yes, Sir!" Harper says with a smile beaming across his face. He salutes one last time and leaves.

"Wow, he's really happy to have the night off," I say turning towards the garden, not ready to face Eli yet.

"His family arrived this morning, he hasn't seen them in months."

"Well that was mighty nice of you, Mr Alutiiq." I turn to face him and lean up against the porch railings.

"Everyone deserves to spend time with their family. Especially when they take such good care of mine." He stops right in front of me.

Family? Oh Maker!

There was something about the way he said "mine" that made my knees buckle. I had to use the railing for support and I could feel my breathing becoming shallower in his presence.

"Are you well, Miss Thomas? You seem a little… *tense*." He says getting as close as he can without touching me. The familiar electricity coupled with the way he said "*tense*" sends a wave of desire running through my body. I can feel my breath catching in my throat and goose pimples cover my skin.

"You look like you need some rest, Miss Thomas. Maybe an early night is in order." He leans his head down so we're now nose to nose.

I lean my head back to look him in the eye. "Yes, some rest would be ideal, Mr Alutiiq, but you see, I believe I have some sort of pest in my room. It kept me awake all night." I let a smile play around my eyes.

"Pest, you say? Really?" he adds a deep chuckle. "I don't recall you complaining at the time?" He leans his hands either side of me on the railing.

"Eli? Boy? Are you out here?" Lady A shouts from the garden room.

Without thinking I grab Eli's arms and feel the now familiar pull from teleporting and within a blink we are both standing in the middle of the woods about a mile out from my family's yard.

His eyes glass over slightly and before I can check on him he falls backwards hitting his head on the moss-covered ground.

"Eli!" I rush to his side and kneel next to him.

"What the Maker just happened?" he says sitting up and rubbing his head.

"I'm so sorry, I did it without thinking."

"Did what? I feel like my guts have been stirred."

"Yeah, sorry. Feels like that the first few times."

"What does?"

"Teleporting."

"What? You were able to take both of us?"

"Apparently," I say sheepishly.

"I didn't even know you could do that."

"Neither did I," I declare slightly embarrassed. "Are you okay?"

"Yeah I think so… Where are we?" he says looking around.

"About a mile out from my folks' place."

"Bought me home to meet the folks huh?" he says with a smirk and a wink.

Sexy idiot.

"Not quite, Big Boy. Actually, I couldn't decide where to go so ended up somewhere in the middle I think."

"What was the other option?"

"I have a spot, about a mile that way," I say pointing towards the lake.

"So, what'll it be, Miss Thomas? Lead the way."

"I think home, don't you? It's going to rain."

"Rain? Are you crazy? It's bright sunshine."

"If you say so…," I say knowing it's going to rain in a few minutes. I always knew when the rain was coming. I loved the rain. Everything about it sang to me. The smell, the sound, the calmness. It gave me joy, where it gave most people the opposite.

"So, are your folks home?" he asks looking a little nervous.

I stop and look up at him with mock shock "Mr Alutiiq… Are you nervous about seeing my parents?" I laugh.

"No! Not nervous, just… Well, I haven't seen them since all this happened. I was under the impression that your father hasn't taken it all that well." He said keeping his eyes straight ahead rather than at me. Now that I come to think of it, I haven't seen them since all this happened, and yeah, I can't imagine my father was taking it all that well at all.

"Yeah, come to think of it, he probably hates you… We should get out of here before he gets the shotgun out." I laugh but he looks a little too serious. "Hey," I say grabbing his hand. "What's up? I was only messing about the shotgun. He probably won't shoot you," I say trying to lighten the mood.

It's raining.

"That's not funny," he says releasing my hand and looking up to the sky.

Told you so!

I must look as hurt as I felt as he instantly grabs my hand again. "I'm Sorry, Evelyn. It's just… It's just that your father needs to approve, he needs to like me."

"Eli, he'll love you because I do, don't worry."

"Evelyn it's not that… What did you just say?" he says finally looking at me. I froze. I hadn't thought about what I was saying and I just blurted out that I loved him.

Well played, Thomas, perfect timing as always!

I didn't know what to say so I just stayed frozen staring up at him like a dear in headlights.

"Evelyn, what did you just say?"

Deep breath, Evie, you can do this.

I let out a long sigh. "I'm sorry," I say looking at my feet. "I know that it's only been a few days really, and I didn't really mean to come out with it that way or at all in fact, it's not really what I meant. You see…"

"So, you're saying you don't love me?"

No… Yes… No! Wait… What was the question again?"

Eloquent as ever, Evelyn.

I still can't bring myself to look him in the eye. I know if I do I'll crumble like an idiot, not that my current method is going any better.

"Evelyn," he says gently, bringing his hand up to my face and cupping my cheek. "Do you love me?" he says, his voice taking on whole new level of sexy gruffness.

"Eli, I…" I still can't look at him, or admit it.

"Evelyn?" He brings his hand under my chin and lifts my head to meet his gaze. "Do you love me?"

I finally give in and look up. We lock eyes and as predicted I crumble. "Yes, Eli. I love you. I have from…" Before I can finish the sentence his lips are on mine. His giant arms wrap around me and pull me into him. I respond, fling my arms around his neck and shoulders and let my fingers find his hair. He lifts me up and I wrap my legs around his waist. He turns and leans me against a nearby tree. The rain is falling heavily now but it doesn't stop him. I can feel his pleasure pulsing between my thighs and it nearly sends me over the edge. I pull him into me and he kisses me harder and faster. His hands roam my body and caress every inch of me. He pulls out of the kiss to run tiny silk kisses down my neck and chest, following the deep plunge of my shirt. His hands come up and caress the sides of my breasts and he traces soft kisses over my exposed flesh. I gasp as his thumbs find my nipples hard and erect under my shirt.

""Eli!" I breathe out as he continues his exquisite torture on my breasts.

He slowly and deliberately lowers his hands to my hips as he runs a line of soft kisses up my neck and to my ear. He takes a moment and I can hear his laboured breaths in my ear. I take the opportunity to run my tongue around his ear. I let out a moan as I put his lobe between my teeth and pull slightly.

"Evelyn," he breathes gripping my hips even tighter and leaning further into me. Our bodies are flush and I feel his hard strong muscles against me, calling for me to remove the barrier of material between us.

He pulls back and locks eyes with me for a moment. Panting he says, "Evelyn, from the moment we first touched, when our eyes met for the first time, I knew. I knew I would love you. Seeing you every night for over two hundred years I knew. But never… Never in a million years would I have imagined feeling like this. I love you, Evelyn, I love you with everything I have, but right now, in this moment and every moment I have shared with you, love isn't enough. It doesn't justifiably describe how I feel about you, how I feel when I'm with you. You are my everything, my Little Witch, and I would willing give you everything I have to give. And yet… That still doesn't seem enough." His gaze falters and he looks down.

"Eli." I cup his face with my hands and bring his gaze to meet mine. "Eli… This seems like a feeble thing to say following that, but… I feel the same. I really do."

We just stare at each other for a while whilst the rain pours down on us. Letting all that's been said sink in. He doesn't seem to know what to say. Maybe because there is nothing left to be said.

I slowly lower my lips so they're just brushing against his, our eyes still locked. He takes a shaky breath.

"Eli-" Before I can say anything more he crushes his lips into mine and kisses me like I've never been kissed before. So much emotion and passion was flowing off of him, wave after wave of desire and love, so much pure, astonishing, love. He pulls back and appears to be trying to say something but I put a finger on his lips. "Shh! Hold on," I breath into him as I wrap myself around him. I feel the familiar pull and we're suddenly in the middle of my room at my parents' house with our bodies still locked together, he stumbles slightly and sets me down trying to get his balance back.

"Sorry, are you okay?"

He just nods and takes a seat on the edge of my bed. He looks around for a moment, I assume working out where we are.

"This is your room?" he says still a little shaky. I bob my head in reply. A giant sexy smile spreads across his face as he looks up at me.

"What? What's that for?" I ask smiling back at him.

He reaches out a hand to me, "I can't just smile now?"

I take his hand and he pulls me to stand in front of him. "Not like that, that smile looks like trouble," I say running my fingers through his hair.

"I don't know what you mean, Miss Thomas. I was just wondering why you chose to bring us here, that's all," he said looking up at me with the sexiest of expressions.

"You're a big boy, My Alutiiq, I'm sure you can figure it out."

His head falls back and he lets out a deep, dirty chuckle.

"I might need a clue," he says looking at me through hooded eyes.

"A clue huh? How's this?" I hitch my skirt and put one knee on the bed and straddle his lap. My hands wrap around his neck, and I take his bottom lip between my teeth and pull slightly before letting go.

"Mm, I think I'm getting it," he says with a smirk, "but I may need a little more help."

I smile at him shaking my head. I push my hands into his chest forcing him to lean back onto his elbows. He looks up at me with the sexiest smile on his face. I gently pull my shirt out from my skirt and very slowly pull it over my head. He looks at me with nothing but pure desire and it lights a fire deep inside me. I slowly step off of him and stand between his legs. I unzip my skirt and deliberately wiggle out of it. I also say a small prayer to thank the Maker that I put on some good underwear today. I stand before him in a black lace matching panty and bra set and my tall black heels. His eyes are heavy with lust and his breathing laboured. I start to crawl up his body lying on the bed and straddle his hips. I rock my hips on his slightly and feel his bulging pleasure underneath me. I lower myself and run my tongue and tiny kisses up his neck to his ear.

"Are we clear?" I breathe into him.

He turns his head to look at me and runs his fingers around my hips following my panty line. His hands find my hips again and he rocks me into him, pushing himself against me. I let out a small gasp of pleasure at the feel of him through our clothes. He brings his hand up to the nap of my neck and pulls me down so our lips meet. He brushes his lips against mine and I can feel him shaking slightly.

"Are you okay?" I ask threw laboured breathes.

"My Little Witch," he says and places a soft kiss on my forehead. "I am beyond okay." With that he pulls me into him and kisses me hard. One hand is in my hair, the other is grabbing my ass and pushing me into him. My head starts to get foggy and I can feel myself being consumed by him.

Right now there is only the two of us in all the worlds.

His lower hand glides up my back and finds my bra, with ease he undoes it and releases my swollen breasts. I let him remove it completely and he just stares at me a moment, taking me all in. Without thinking I instinctively pull my bottom lip between my teeth. His eyes dart to it and a sexier than sin smile spreads across his face and a growl escapes his chest. Within a flash he flips me onto my back and he is now above me. He waits for me to find his eyes before his hands makes a torturous decent down my body. He lets his fingers fall over my breasts, finding my erect nipple between his thumb and forefinger he rolls it gently sending waves of pleasure through me. I can't help but let my eyes close and my head roll back slightly. But as I do he stops. I look up to see what has caused the agonising lack of contact and as soon as my eyes meet his he starts again. This time his eyes are burning into me, he won't let me look away. No matter how much pleasure rushes through me our eyes stay locked. Leaving my throbbing nipples for a moment his hands now venture down my torso towards my hips. He stops at the lace lining my thighs and runs his fingers under and along the edge until he reaches the back. He grips the back of my thighs and parts my legs. His stare burns into me, his beast is starting to show and his eyes are becoming dark and primal. He needs this as much as I do and the intensity between us is intoxicating.

He slowly runs his hand up my thigh and over my hot centre. Staying atop my panties he starts to massage my core, sending lightning bolts of electricity and pleasure through my entire body. My back arches with pleasure and I long to feel him against my flesh. I go to reach up and pull him down to meet my lips but his free hand grabs my wrists and holds them firmly over my head. Our eyes still locked he continues his exquisite torture of my centre and I buck and arch with intense pleasure.

Maker, he hasn't even touched me yet!

I slowly start to feel the build of hot fire growing in my core and he seems to feel it too as his skilled hands increase their speed and precision. I feel my whole body start to sing with fire and electricity and it all starts to flow towards my hot centre. Small moans start to escape my lips, and unable to take the pleasure anymore I rock my hips in time to his hands. With intense fire brimming at my core I bite down on my bottom lip and let out a loud long moan as it starts to escape me. My whole body bucks and arches at his command and I feel the sweet release fall over me as I find my climax.

My chest heaving and my body still alight with pleasure he finally releases my stare and brings his lips gently to mine. I fling my arms around his neck and let my fingers find his hair. I pull him into me tightly and kiss him with intense appreciation. After a while he pulls out of the kiss and starts laying soft gentle kisses down my neck, following down over my breast, and letting his teeth find my nipples. He then descends further down over my belly button and looks up at me from my between my legs with heavily hooded eyes.

Oh Maker help me!

This look alone is enough to floor me. My breath catches as I exhale and he gives me the sexiest smile I've ever seen. Standing up in front of me he slowly starts to remove my underwear and drops it to the floor next to him. I'm now completely naked apart from my heels, which he decides to leave on. He examines every inch of my body with a serious look on his face. After a while he looks up and meets my gaze.

"Problem?" I ask raising my eyebrows at him.

"Not even close, my Little Witch. Not even close," he says looking at me with complete adoration.

"Good." I smile, "Your turn."

I have to take a deep breath to prepare myself.

He slowly pulls his shirt over his head. His perfectly ripped torso calls out for me to touch it. I long to feel him against me but he continues his maddeningly slow unveiling.

He now reaches for his belt buckle and starts to open it. I push myself forward to sit in front of him on the bed and stop him. He looks at me with a confused expression. I move his hands out of the way and start to unbuckle his belt myself, all the while still looking up into his eyes. I unzip his jeans and let then fall to the floor. He steps out of them and kicks them aside. The golden Adonis stands before me in nothing but his boxers and I can't wait to reveal what's underneath. I run my fingers along the waist band and slowly pull then down, revealing the deep V that sits between his hips, until they fall to the floor leaving him gloriously naked in front of me. I take a moment to take him all in, and there is an awful lot to take in. His ripped chest is heavy with laboured breaths, his eight-pack torso is glistening with sweat and taught, and his perfectly formed V that sits over his hips is blazing the trail to his flawless manhood and strong, thick thighs. My heart skips a beat taking him all in and I feel my breath hitching in my throat. I finally let me eye level rise and find him staring down at me with a smirk on his face.

"Adequate?" he asks gesturing to himself.

I know he's being playful but I can't even begin to think of words. My body and mind have been consumed by the god in front of me so I answer the only way I can think of.

I drop to my knees in front of him and take his exquisite erection in my hand. I would have to use both my hands to hold him fully.

Oh maker!

But for now I just let one hand glide up and down his length before taking him in my mouth. He lets out a deep moan and a growl forms in his chest.

"I'll take that as a yes then," he rumbles looking down at me. I just respond by looking up to meet his gaze and taking him further and faster in my mouth. He moans and growls repeatedly with pleasure, letting me know my efforts are very much appreciated. After a while I quicken my pace and he stiffens in my grip. He reaches down and grabs me by the arms and lifts me onto my feet. I search his eyes, worrying that I did something wrong, but I instantly see that his desire for me has consumed him as mine had. He pushes himself into me and his lips crash into mine. Holding my head and thighs he lowers me onto the bed and climbs on top of me. I part my legs and wrap them around him. He takes a moment to hold my gaze as his pulsing erection finds my centre. He pauses, letting himself rest against my hot core. With my hands in his hair we share a knowing and loving look that tells us what is about to happen. Our mating bond is about to be united, now becoming final and unbreakable. Making me his and him mine, forever.

He holds my gaze and I feel him start to slowly enter me. The feel of my core stretching to accommodate him is intoxicating and I let a long, low moan of pleasure. He enters me fully and lets me adjust to his size. The feeling of him finally inside me sends endless waves of electricity and pleasure pulsing through my body and I can already feel the fire flowing towards my core. He pulls out almost all the way and slowly enters me again, this time letting himself fully enjoy the motion. His head falls back and a deep growl escapes his lips. He slowly and purposefully moves himself in and out of me. Feeling every inch of him fill me over and over again has my head spinning and it isn't long before I'm yearning for more. More speed, more pressure, more him.

I tighten my legs around his waist and let him know my desires. He doesn't disappoint. He starts to build his momentum and I arch my back and rock my hips in time with his.

With our heads buried in each other's necks and moans and growls getting louder and longer he picks up the pace even more. I feel a deep hot fire rushing towards my core as he moves inside me. As I start to feel the beginnings of my release heading for my centre I grips his hair and pull his head up to meet my gaze. Our eyes lock and the pleasure and joy in his eyes are my undoing. I keep my eyes on his as I feel the fire reach my core and explode. Just as my climax peaks I feel his hit him at the same time. His body stiffens around me sending me into even more of a heady climax than before and we both moan and growl

out in perfect, unbelievable pleasure, moving as one until
our ecstasy comes to a sweet and extraordinary end.

Chapter Twenty-Nine

I wake what must be hours later to the most incredible feeling. I'm wrapped in his arms and lying on his chest with his heart beating like music in my ear. I snuggle into him some more not wanting this moment to end.

"Hey there, my sexy Little Witch." His voice gravelly from sleep, "how are you feeling?" He kisses the top of my head and holds me tight.

"Good," I say grinning from ear to ear.

"Good?" he asks with a chuckle. "That was the best morning of my life and you feel good?" He rolls me over and kisses my softly.

I hug him tightly and whisper in his ear, "I feel better than I could ever describe, Eli. I've never felt so complete."

"Good," he says raising his eyebrows and giving me a mocking smile, "so, what would you like to do for the rest of the day?"

"Do? Shouldn't we be getting back? Charlton will worry, no?"

"It's not every day you unite with your mate, Evelyn. I think he'll manage on his own for a while."

"Well, in that case…" I climb on top of him and we fall victim to another round of glorious love making.

After about an hour my stomach is growling like a grizzly so he insists that we get some food. No one should be home at this time of day so I head downstairs in his t-shirt while he freshens up. I bounce into the kitchen and head for the fridge knowing that they'll be some good leftovers tucked away in there. Momma never knew how to throw away good food.

Which I definitely inherited.

I rummage for a while in the depths of the fridge when I feel warm giant arms wrap around me.

"What's cooking, good looking?" he growls in my ear.

"Seriously? What's cooking, good looking? What are you, eight hundred?" I tease.

"Hey, now, don't mock your elders," he says playfully whilst tracing soft kisses up and down my neck.

I turn around in his arms and meet his lips with mine. Being here in my home with him was overwhelmingly good. That added to being able to forget for a moment all that was going on in reality and just be us, was an intoxicating mix. We kiss each other hard and passionately until I hear a tiny cough. My body froze. Once he realised why I'd stopped he was off me in a flash and I looked up to see my entire family standing at the patio doors staring at us and giggling. Well, all giggling apart from my father that is. He face was cold and stern and even when my whole body flushed a deep crimson and I tried to look away in horror his gaze never faltered.

Jimmy was the first in the door. "Afternoon, Sis! Good morning, I take it?" He gave me a smug wink and walked over to Eli. "Good morning, Mr Alutiiq. So nice of you stop by. Here for the party I presume?"

"Party? What party?" I ask, confused.

"Evelyn Thomas!" my mother yells. "What party?" She brings me in for a hug and whispers in my ear, "you better talk to your father, he's been driving himself senseless this last week." She puts me at arm's length and loses the whisper. "Have you been away so long you forgot your birthday? It's Vesper-Hain!"

I can't believe I didn't realise. Things had flown by back at The Lodge and I hadn't even given it a single thought. It's my birthday. I look over to Eli, whom to my surprise, is looking hurt and angry with me.

Suddenly the kitchen is full with my family and everyone is bustling about and introducing themselves to Eli, who of course is acting like the perfect gentleman, even though he's shirtless and uncomfortable. My mother starts prepping food for the evening's festivities and I signal to Eli that I'll be back shortly. I see him offer his services to my mother who takes him up on it gratefully. She passes him vegetables to chop just before I duck out to the yard and find my father sitting on the porch swing.

He keeps his eyes straight ahead but I can see he's pissed. I sheepishly walk over to the swing and sit next to him, "Hey, Dad." I can't bring myself to look at him yet, so I let my eyes wonder over the yard and surrounding trees. "Dad I'm sorry about before. If I'd have known anyone was home I wouldn't have… You know…"

"Evelyn Thomas. If you think for one for minute that that is the problem then you don't know me at all," he barks. "You leave from here in a less than okay state and we don't hear from you for all this time. All we get is some half-assed information from some strange doctor who shows up here telling us some crazy cock'n'ball story about succubae and how you're in danger. We deserve more than that, Evelyn. I was worried sick about you. And now you just show up here out of the blue, smooching some giant in the kitchen like nothing is wrong…I don't know what to say, kid, I really don't."

"Dad," is all I can muster before floods of tears fall from my eyes. It's feels like it's been ages since I'd seen my father and I missed him so much. Underneath everything that had been going on I really was scared for what might happen. I wanted to come home and talk with him, feel safe with him, like I had as a kid, but Charlton said it was best to stay away. For their safety as much as I my own. I felt the stress and fear of the last few weeks fall out of me in heaving sobs. I feel my dad's arm drop over my shoulder and he pulls me in to him and just holds me while I sob. After a while my sobs die down a little, "Dad… I'm so, sorry!" I say trying to wipe the continuous tears from my eyes. "I never meant to leave you out of all this. I wanted to come home, but they said it would be safer for you if I stayed away." I tried to control the tears but it was useless, they started to flood again.

"Now, now, Kiddo. It's all over," he says hugging me again and stroking my hair. "I was so cross with you, I still am. But as long as you're safe and home, all is right with the world." My crying eases and he pulls back to look at me. "Finally done then is it?" he says smirking.

"Done? What do you mean?" I ask still holding back tears.

"Well, I see you and Mr Alutiiq are back on, are you not?"

I blush from head to toe and avert my eyes.

Done? What the Maker?

"Oh, Evelyn, you're a grown woman, more grown than most when they meet their mate. There's no need to be shy about it, it's the most natural thing in the world, kiddo." he says rubbing my back. "He must be quite a feller though, eh? To be worthy of you."

"Dad," is again all I can muster before being overcome by more sobs.

"Oh, Kiddo!" he sighs pulling me in for a hug. "Is everything okay?"

"Yeah, everything's fine." I lie, not wanting to worry him further. "I guess I just didn't realise how overwhelmed I was. I'm so sorry."

"Poppycock! That's what your old dad's here for, Kiddo." He plants a quick kiss on the top of my head and gets to his feet. "Right then, kid. Can't sit around here all day. We've got a party to sort." He gives me a wink, pats my head and disappears inside. My eyes follow to where dad left and Eli is making his way over.

"Sorry, I didn't mean to interrupt." he says hanging back.

I must look wonderful.

I shift a little uncomfortably in my chair, realising that I'm still in his t-shirt and nothing else I must look terrible after sobbing for the last ten minutes.

"Are you okay, my Little Witch?" he says kneeling in front of me and cupping my hands with his. I just stare into his beautiful face, wondering how this exquisite creature could be meant for me.

"Evelyn? Is everything okay?"

I close my eyes and try to find a connection with his mind. Once I think he'll be able to *"**hear**"* me, I open my eyes and lock them with his. I concentrate on the connection and push all that I feel for him through it. It's difficult at first so I close my eyes again to help try and ease it, and then it just flows. I feel everything I have pouring into him, showing him just how astonishing he is and how much he means to me already, how much he has meant to me for all these years.

When I open my eyes his are filled with tears.

"Eli, I'm sorry I…" before I can finish his lips are on mine.

Maker I love it when he does that!

He kisses me so tenderly but so passionately at the same time. I can feel his love for me in this kiss and I can also feel the gratitude for showing him how I feel. After a while he pulls back slightly and brushes my nose with his.

"Evelyn Thomas, thank you for making me the happiest man alive. If I could do the same for you I would. I swear I will find a way to show how I feel, Evie."

"You do, Eli. Every moment we're together."

"I do?" he looks at me a little confused.

"Whenever we're together I can feel you. I feel what you feel. Your emotions flow off of you in waves. You're so open to me, and I know… I know how you feel because you show me every time you're near me… Sometimes even when you're not," I joke.

"When I'm not?"

"I was able to connect to you from a distance one time. I'm sorry, it wasn't on purpose as such, and I didn't know I could do it then. It was the first night you came here actually." I say smiling in memory of it.

"Oh," he says beaming at me and then quickly averting his eyes and feeling ashamed.

"No, please, Eli. Let's not worry about that today. I don't want to think of reality right now. Let's just be here." The last thing I needed was to drag up past (or present) issues.

His gaze meets mine again and he furrows his brow. "So, it's your birthday?" he asks looking cross with me.

"Oh… Yes. Well it's actually tomorrow, but we always celebrate today, you know… Easier and all that… Why?"

"Why? Do you not think I should know when your birthday is?"

"Sorry I guess I just never thought about it. I never really do… I've had a few too many to worry about them now."

"Evelyn Thomas, why would you not celebrate your birthday?"

Why does everyone keep using my full name!?

"Because, *Mr Alutiiq*, I've had over 230 of them and it gets a little same-y"

"Well, that changes now, my Little Witch. From now on we celebrate your birthday."

"That really isn't necessary."

"Evelyn Thomas, as far as I'm concerned you being born is the biggest reason to celebrate ever! Now shut up whining and let's get ready to celebrate the best thing that ever happened to me… Shall we?" He finishes holding out his hand for me. I couldn't help but smile, it was hard to keep whining when someone so perfect loved you so much.

We made our way back though the kitchen where mom declared I should keep him around as he could cook and had a body to die for. Although she was stating the absolute truth it didn't help my embarrassment.

Yay, finally on the end of embarrassing parent moments.

We manage to escape my mother in the kitchen just to be met by Jimmy at the foot of the stairs. He had a look on his face that was far too smug for my liking.

"Hey, Sis, where we off to? Heading upstairs are we?" he winks.

I try and give him the buzz off look but he just ignores me. Eli, standing tall over both of us suddenly sticks out his hand to shakes Jimmy's. Jimmy follows suit and shakes his hand, I don't think he knew what was going on though.

"Jimmy, I owe you an apology. I'm deeply sorry for what transpired that night, between the two of us. I hope you can find it in you to excuse my behaviour and to accept my sincerest apologies and my further apologies for taking so long to do this?" He just stands there staring at him looking and feeling completely earnest.

Jimmy just looks at him in shock. "Well. I have to say, I didn't expect that. But it's water under the bridge, as they say. And it looks as though we're family now, so… It's normal, right? Families fight?" he says bobbing his head at both of us. "But don't beat yourself up about it, Charlton explained everything the following day, we've just been waiting for you two to catch up." He chucks me a wink and just struts off.

Are my family at all normal?

Eli just smiles and starts for the stairs.

"I'm sorry, he just…"

"Sorry? What for? I like him. I think he and Charlton are a great fit." He declares as he heads upstairs.

"Wait… What?" I chase up after him. "What do you mean him and Charlton?"

"They're a thing are they not?"

"Are they?" I shout. "Do I literally not see anything? How did I not know that? … But Charlton's married?" I add in shock.

"So? … Look it's what I said to you before, Evelyn, it's not like you imagine it. It's only politics. Nothing more."

"Well, there you go." I sit and think about the two of them for a moment. "I'm so happy for them. Now that I think about it, they'd be so ridiculously great together."

"They are," he adds heading for my En-suite.

"What? You've seen them together? Why didn't you tell me?"

"It wasn't my business to tell." He adds simply.

"Mr Alutiiq, we are going to have to work on your communication skills if this is going to work… You can't just hold back information like that!" I declare.

Suddenly he's right in front of me staring down at me through hooded eyes.

"*If*, this is going to work?" he growls, emphasizing the *if*.

I swallow hard, suddenly becoming very heady under his glare. "Did I say *if*?" I get out through a nervous giggle.

He smirks at me and picks me up in his arms. "What are we going to do with you, Miss Thomas?" he says carrying me to the En-suite.

I fling my arms around his neck and raise my eyebrows at him. "I have some requests."

He just growls and hauls me to the bathroom.

We spend a few hours making steamy love in the shower and then getting ready for the evening's festivities.

He slips back in to the clothes he was wearing earlier and I pick out a pair of skinny jeans and a t-shirt. I feel a bit casual but it's comfy and that seems about right for tonight. I consider a jacket as it's a little chilly, but looking up at the giant bear at my side I figure I wouldn't need it. There'll for sure be a fire pit outside as well, Dad never has a party without a fire pit.

When we finally head downstairs the party is already in full swing. There must be a good twenty people dotted inside the house, and that's just the stragglers.

We head to the kitchen where mom is still fussing over food and to my surprise is being aided by Charlton.

"Ah! The chef has arrived!" Mom yells over the top of all the hustle and bustle.

"Ah yes, I feel my brother would be much better suited to this roll. I'm afraid cooking isn't one of my strong points," Charlton adds taking off the piny my mother has obviously forced him to wear and passing it to Eli.

"Yeah, Charlie here isn't much of a cook," she adds with a grimace.

Charlie?

"It would be my pleasure, Mrs Thomas. What can I do?" Eli, asks as my mother beams at him. She chucks me a wink, "He's definitely a keeper, Kiddo."

"Are you sure? I hear bears can be handful," Jimmy adds with a chuckle as he comes through the back door. Charlton immediately looks a little uncomfortable.

Odd.

Charlton heads over to me, turns me away from the crowd, "could I possibly have a minute of your time?" he asks very seriously so only I can hear him. I just nod in response. I'm assume this is going to be a telling off for disappearing today, but as I follow him outside and to a secluded corner of the yard he turns to look at me with what looks and feels like fear coming off of him.

"Charlton what is it? Is everything okay?" the look in his eyes sends a shiver of panic over me.

"Well, that depends. Miss Thomas, I'm afraid I haven't been completely honest with you these last few days. That's not to say I've lied, just that I've been withholding information from you."

My heart sinks. "What is it, Charlton? What's going on?"

"Well, now before we get into it, I feel you should know that our friendship, although it's only been a short while, has come to mean a lot to me, especially with your union to Eli pending…" He stops dead and looks me right in the eye. "Oh my goodness. It's complete isn't it? You're united aren't you?" he says eyes wide.

"Charlton you're starting to freak me out, what's going on?" But he doesn't answer he just stares at me. "Charlton?" I demand and he responds by picking me up and hugging me tight.

"Oh Maker! I couldn't be happier for you both! This truly is a joyous occasion!"

He sets me down and is beaming from ear to ear. "How do you feel? How are your powers? Have they kicked in yet? Sometimes it takes a few days."

"Charlton! I feel great and no they haven't. Now can you focus please!? What's wrong?"

"Oh, right. Sorry I get a little carried away sometimes. Miss Thomas, I need to ask you something and I need you to be completely honest with me… Can you do that for me?"

"Of course, what is it?" I ask with worry.

"Miss Thomas, will you grant me the privilege of blessing a relationship between me and your brother?"

What?

I just stare at him, completely confused.

He seems to panic at my response. "Now I know we are not bonded in anyway, but we have come to care for one another in this short time, but he has made his wishes very clear I agree with him completely. If you are not happy with the idea of us being involved then I will step aside immediately," he says holding his hands up and shaking his head.

"Charlton I don't understand?" I say staring at him, my eyes a bit glazed over. "Why would it matter what I think?"

"Your brother has made his wishes very clear. If we wanted this to go any further then we had to clear it with you."

"But… Why?"

"Because you're true family to him, Miss Thomas. Your blessing means everything," he says gently.

I continue to stare at him for some time and I think my lack of words starts to make him uncomfortable.

"Charlton, I… I don't know what to say?"

"I understand, Miss Thomas. Thank you for your time," he turns to leave.

"Charlton, no! Please wait. You misunderstand me," I say closing my eyes and shaking my head, trying to clear the confusion from it. "Charlton I only don't know what to say to Jimmy's wishes. As for my blessing, you of course have it. I couldn't think of a single person in this world better suited to my brother. I mean he is a complete pain in the ass, but he also a one in a million… As are you. I know we haven't known each other very long, at all really, but I feel your heart, Charlton, and from what I know, you're a wonderful man… Bear." I add with a smile for good measure.

Charlton looks down at me with tears in his eyes. "You are truly a beautiful lady, Miss Thomas. I don't know how to thank you enough!"

"Just look after my brother," I say smiling up at him. "He's far more delicate than he makes out. And stop calling me Miss Thomas!" I scold.

"Apologies, Evelyn, and I will do my best. But I fret that he is the one looking after me," he adds in a whisper. He brings me in for another hug and we make our way back to the house to find both boys sitting around a table outside with a few beers in hand.

"There she is," Jimmy shouts. "Lady of the hour."

I blush from head to toe. "Thanks for that," I say shooting a dirty look at him.

"Is it time for Evie's birthday cake yet, Mar?" he shouts at the top of his lungs and laughs.

"You're such an ass!" I say hitting him on the arm. "See what I mean?" I say to Charlton. "Are you sure you want to get involved with this idiot?" I tease.

"Ah, so you two had the talk huh?" Jimmy asks looking between the two of us. "So what's the verdict, Sis?"

"I told him he could do better," I say laughing. "You're a pain in the ass and you're not house trained." Everyone laughs along with me.

"Coming from the girl who used pee her pants every time she had a bad dream! Look out, Eli, you never know when she might lose it again."

"Shut up!" I yell at him "It only happened one time." Everybody laughs, including me.

We spent the next few hours talking and laughing together, it was quite easily the best time of my life. I couldn't remember a time I'd felt so at ease or had so much fun. My heart was bursting with joy. I had my beautiful family and their many friends celebrating my birthday, and it was topped off with my new family, my two new bear additions. One was one of the sweetest men I'd ever met and the other had become my heart and soul in the space of two weeks. Looking around this table alone my heart could burst with pride and joy, I couldn't think of anywhere else in the world I'd rather be.

Chapter Thirty

After a few too many beers between us and endless laughter, my dad approached the table.

"Hey, Kids, how goes it? All having a good time I hope?" he says clamping a hand down on Eli's shoulder.

"Yes, Dad. We're having a great time. Well I am anyway," I say beaming from ear to ear.

"Yeah, all good, Dad. You?" Jimmy asks.

"Yes, Son, yes. It's a great turn out this year. Everyone seems to be having a ball," he shifts oddly and looks around the party for a moment. "Would it be okay if I borrowed young Eli here, for a moment? We have some business to discuss."

I look at him a little confused. But before I can interject, Eli is up and out of his chair and preparing to follow my father.

"I won't keep him long, promise," my father adds before walking off.

"Don't go anywhere, my Little Witch," Eli growls in my ear as he bends down to kiss my cheek before turning to follow my father.

I let my eyes follow them as they disappear into the crowd. When I turn back, both Jimmy and Charlton are grinning at me.

"What?" I asks a little startled.

"What? What do you mean, what? He's totally getting the talk!"

"The talk? What's "the talk"?"

"The look after my daughter talk, Dummy," Jimmy adds flicking a bottle top at me.

"Hey," I say batting it away, "why is that happening? Make it stop!" I say trying to get up and see where they have gone.

"Not in a million years, little Sis. It's Dad's right… And maybe he should hear it."

"What's that supposed to mean?" I shoot him daggers.

"I only mean, he should here how important you are to all of us, and how he won't live a day if he ever hurts you."

"Oh, Jimmy! You're so overdramatic."

"Now, Evelyn, I have to agree with your brother. As much as I know what you mean to Eli, it is your father's right to give him "the talk" as it were."

"Fine! You two gang up on me," I say getting to my feet. "I'm getting a drink, anybody want one?"

"Yes," they both say in unison and laugh about it.

I leave them to their privacy and go to hunt down some beers.

On my way to the kitchen I see Eli and my father hunched together and talking intensely in a far corner of the yard at the other side of the house. I let my father have his moment and leave them to it.

Just before heading inside something from the trees at the end of the yard catches my eye. It's Anna-May and she's waving at me like a crazy person. I drop the empty beer bottles I was carrying on a nearby table and make my way over to her.

"Hay, Little Lady. What's up?" I say as soon as I'm in earshot. But she doesn't reply she just gesture for me to come over to her.

I reach her and hold out my hand to grab her shoulder and that's when I feel it. It isn't Anna-May at all. I freeze on the spot, my heart pounds in my chest and I can feel the blood leaving my face.

Then suddenly I can feel them, all of them. Buried in the darkness of the trees I feel at least fifteen succubae spread out around the perimeter of the yard. My heart sinks. The version of Anna-May in front of me slowly backs into the trees and stops just before she's out of sight. "Come quietly or we'll join the party," she says in her sweet tone, although this version has a coldness to it that sends a chill up my spine.

I look back at the party in full swing, all my friends and loved ones, chatting and laughing. I consider screaming for Eli, but that would put my whole family in danger. I have to get them away from here, far away from here. So, I do the only thing I can think of… I run.

As fast as my legs will carry me I run into the trees. I can feel them closing in around me but I keep going and they follow. I feel a new power growing in my limbs, I move almost at a super speed, I can feel them getting left behind and as much as this makes me feel safer I fear for my family's safety so I slow slightly, letting them catch up. Somehow I manage to over judge it and let them get too close and that's when it hits me, an over powering pain. It starts deep in my chest and spreads like searing hot lava. I clutch at my chest and feel myself losing my footing. I stumble slightly and have to teleport a few feet in front of me to stop myself hitting the ground.

The pain is now coursing through my body, it feels like hot acid is running through my veins. I have to teleport a few more times until I reach the clearing by the lake. I try to make it to the water's edge but my body gives out before I get there.

I fall to the ground with a thud and clutch both hands to my chest which now feels like it may burst open at any minute. I scream out in shear agony, the pain overpowering all my senses.

It finally eases off a little and there's a tall figure standing over me. He kneels down and grabs my face in his hand. "Such a waste," he snarls at me. "You would have been a fine breeder, Witch." His voice is cold and dark and his choice of words sends a surge of anger through my body and I fight against his grip, but he just laughs at me. "You may be powerful enough to hold off one of us, my pet, but you stand no chance with a whole clan." He nods to one of the others and another wave of pain rushes through my body. I scream out again and feel my body sag over once it ends.

I want to stand and fight, or run, or anything, but my body is in so much pain I can barely move. The one beside me grabs my face again. "Now, how shall we do this, pet?" he says running a knife down the side of my cheek. "Now don't look so confused. You see, you could have come quietly the first time and we would have just used you for breeding. But, no. You had to play hard to get and now we have new orders. You see, there's a bounty on your head, my pretty, a big one. I don't know what you did or who you pissed off, but I also don't care. We're just following orders and reaping a big fat reward in the process." I hear the others laugh and cheer from all around us.

He angles my face so he can look me right in the eye and he suddenly looks startled and drops my face. "What are you?" he shouts.

I look at him confused and then remember my eyes, last time I was this angry my eyes glowed. I figured I must be doing it now. He takes a few steps away from me.

"Enough wasting time." I hear a woman's voice shout from behind me, "Finish her!"

"She's no witch, look at her!" shouts the one in front of me.

I think for a moment. He's right. I am no witch, not like any I've ever met anyway. I was much more powerful and had many more abilities to boot. I think for a moment and try to recall anything that might help me now. At first I can't think of a single thing, but then through the panic I remember a feeling I had once. It was during the hearing with Lady A. I felt like I could suck up all the energy around me and blast it at her. I had no idea if I could do it or not but it felt possible at the time, so it made sense to at least try it now.

Keeping low I slowly get to my knees. I concentrate on all the energy around me, some from them and some from the elements. I can feel my body start to absorb it. I dig my hands into the ground and gather as much power as I can. I hear them start to murmur around me.

"What's she doing?" "What is that?"

I feel them start to send bolts of energy towards me but this time, instead of feeling torturous agony, my body seems to absorb it. I soak up as much as I can before I feel myself lift off the ground and levitate in mid-air. When I open my eyes I see my whole body is now glowing. I look straight at the succubae in front of me and imagine pushing all my energy into him. As soon as I can feel everything focus and centre I push. I force everything I have at him.

A bright white beam of light shoots out of my body and into his. At first he looks down at it and seems confused by what is happening. But then his face starts to distort. He suddenly lets out a blood curdling scream and his body is lifted into the air like mine. His screams fill the space around us but I don't stop. I continue to push everything I have at him until suddenly his body ignites into bright blue and white flames. His body is consumed by the flames and within seconds he is gone. Turned into nothing but dust. I feel an emptiness fill me and I fall back to the ground.

"She killed him." I hear one of them shout.

"She's no witch!"

"Let's get out of here!"

"No! We have a job to do. That's two of us she's killed now. It's time we end her!"

I want to retaliate, I want to run, scream, anything, but I have nothing. I used what reserve I had on annihilating their leader, I have nothing left for the rest of them.

I sag over onto the cold hard ground residing myself to my fate. I think of how wonderful the day has been and pray to the Maker to watch over Eli and my family and I close my eyes and wait.

Once my eyes are closed I can see him.

Eli!

That's when it hits me. Am I really just going to roll over and die, just like that? I have waited centuries for a day like today and I'm not going to settle for just one. I want to share my life with Eli, I have to do something.

I search my body, I search my soul. Looking for even a scrap of energy that might be left. Anything that might help me last long enough to think of a way out of here. And suddenly I feel it. That familiar electricity. He isn't near but I can feel him, almost as if I can tap into his energy from afar. My body starts to spring to life. Each muscle comes back to me one by one. I open my eyes and see them forming a circle around me. I focus my efforts. I think to myself, just one burst of energy and that should be enough to run to the water, then I should be able to use its power to help me fight. I bring my body into myself and clench everything I have in concentration. Suddenly I feel myself release, sending streaming bolts of white light flying in all directions.

I hear them scream out in pain and figure this is my chance, I struggle to my feet. I only get a few feet towards the water before I am overcome with agonising pain again.

Worse this time. My body convulses and spasms on the ground and I am paralysed. I can barely think straight, let alone move. My limbs are no longer my own and I scream out in pure pain. My whole body is consumed by it.

I'm suddenly flipped onto my back and another surge of pain floods my body. A woman is standing over me and laughing. "You're a feisty little fucker, I'll give you that," she says putting her foot on my throat. "But enough is enough." She pushes her foot down onto my throat and holds her hand out for someone to pass her something. A sliver of silver appears in her hand and she leans down over me.

"Time to say goodnight, little bitch!" she raises the knife above her head and winks at me.

I close my eyes and focus everything I have on Eli, I try to find a connection. I have to let him know one last time how happy he's made me, even if just for one day. I frantically search for him and as soon as I find him I lose him again. I don't have the energy to hold on to the connection.

A single tear rolls down my cheek and I open my eyes to meet hers.

"That's better, I like to look into the eyes as the life leaves the body. More fun that way," she laughs. She quickly pulls her arms back and plunges her knife deep into my stomach.

Just as her knife breaks the skin above my belly button the sky lights up with an amazing flash of lightening. I have to close my eyes to the glaring brightness. When I open them again a giant bolt of lightning has hit the ground a few feet away from me and is coming down in a continuous stream. The succubae all around me start to panic and shout when suddenly several bolts fly out of the main stream and connects with each succubae, including the one above me. I can hear horrific screams and what sounds like wood crackling on a fire, I watch in horror as the woman above me is electrocuted alive by the bolt of lightning streaming from the main bolt hitting the ground a few feet away.

She shakes uncontrollable and her body is burning inside out.

After what feels like ages she finally bursts into a cloud of dust and it floats gently over me in a small gust of wind and then everything falls silent.

I lay my head back on the grass beneath me for a moment before deciding to use what energy I have left to get out of here.

I raise myself up onto my elbows and see steaming patches of grass around me. I scan the area quickly to see if anyone is still around. I don't see anything so try to get to my feet. I stumble at the first try, the deep wound in my stomach is bleeding profusely and I'm still running on empty.

I manage to get onto my knees when I see something move in the distance.

In the spot the lightning had struck a figure now stood. Tall and slender. I froze.

Slowly but purposefully it walked towards me. It wasn't until it was in front of me that I could see him properly.

His dark skin was like porcelain. He was tall and slender and positively beautiful. Almost breath-taking.

He walked over and stood in front of me, he seemed to examine me for a moment.

He knelt before me and held out his hand.

I backed away from him like a feral animal.

"I will not hurt you, Evelyn. Come let us get you home." His voice was strong but soft, it comforted me as though it was familiar. But still I hesitated. I've never seen or heard of anything with such power in my life, and I had no idea who he was or how he knew my name. I just stared up at him.

"Come, Evelyn. This is no place for you. Let us leave it now."

Reluctantly I went to hold my hand out to him but it sent a shooting pain though my body from the wound in my stomach. I doubled over with a scream.

"You are hurt?" he said rushing to my side to examine me. He pushed me backwards on to the ground and placed his hands over my wound. A white glow appeared under his hands and after a few moments the pain was gone and I was left with nothing but a warm, tingling feeling where the wound should have been. I ran my hand over my stomach and looked up at him in amazement. I'd seen some healers in my time but never anything like this.

What are you?

"I will answer all your question later, Evelyn. But please, let us leave here," he said as if reading my mind. He holds out his hand for me again and this time I take it.

As our hands touch a beautiful patterned rope of silver and gold light appear around them. It's mesmerizingly beautiful and it wisps around our hands as though it's dancing. Suddenly with a flash of light it tightens around us and burns into my skin. I try to pull my hand away from the pain but he holds it in place and brings his other hand over the top of mine.

"It will only hurt for a moment, Evelyn. I've been waiting centuries to find you, I would never do anything to hurt you, my Princess." He smiles down at me sweetly and I feel an almost familiar wave of contentment wash over me.

He lowers his head and kisses my hand. As he does I hear a deep growl come from the edge of the trees nearby and feel the familiar electricity run though my body.

Eli!

The only thing that could be seen through the darkness were glowing red eyes and giant rolling shoulders. He slowly makes his way over to us and stands over me looking down at the stranger. He looks down at me for a moment and then back to the man as a low growl starts to form in his chest, but it wasn't a threatening one, he seemed to be thanking him. The stranger just bows his head, looks between the two of us and vanishes into thin air. I can't seem to stop staring at the spot he left. There was something oddly familiar about him, something that reminded me of home, just not a home I'd ever known.

Eli laid down on the grass next to me and gestured for me to get on his back, I did as I was instructed. As he carried me back to the house I couldn't help but lean over into his deep fur and take a deep breath of his intoxicating sent, he showed his appreciation with a purr-like rumble in his chest. As I lay on his back surrounded by him and his scent all I could think was that whomever that man was or wherever he'd come from, this was my home now. The beautiful man and powerful bear beneath was my home, and I never want to be anywhere else ever again.

I would like to take this opportunity to thank you for reading the first instalment of Evelyn's story.

I sincerely hope you enjoyed it and would love to hear your thoughts.

You can contact me via www.westrm.com and of course your feedback on Amazon is always welcome.

You can also visit www.westrm.com to subscribe to the mailing list and be the first to hear about future publications and the release of book two.

I look forward to hearing from you.